The Chronicles of Origin

Rise of Ares
Part 2

Aron Taylor

WIZARD'S KEEP PUBLISHING

For information contact :
Wizard's Keep Publishing
http://www.wizardskeeppublishing.com
email: info@wizardskeeppublishing.com

ISBN: 978-1-945737-08-4(paperback)
      978-1-945737-09-1(hardcover)
      978-1-945737-10-7(ebook)

LCCN: 2016947906

Cover Design by Josh Tam
http://joshtam.net

First Edition: October 2016

10 9 8 7 6 5 4 3 2 1

Dedicated to My Son
Michael

\

BLUE MARBLE

With several events occurring simultaneously unseen forces were at play. Nergal, lead of the Seraphim who were reptilians seeking retribution for centuries of confinement at the hands of the Nephilim. Nergal's grey's covered the planet Simud which was also Mars obtaining the only material, gold, that the Nephilim would be willing to for genetic material. In the coming battles Nergal choosing Tiamat which would later become Ceres, the temporary home of the Nephilim as the new home to the Seraphim after trading the DNA of Michael to the Nephilim.

Nergal's species were the former rulers of the universe known as the Carian Empire inhabiting a specific area of the universe known as The House of Aln on the planet Venus. Individuals within the Carian Empire were called Iln. Tiamat the future home of the Carian Empire to avenge the former destruction of that great civilization sending the Nephilim to the planet Gia also known as Earth.

The Nephilim are ancient outcasts of a universe outside this reality. Abandoned on a dying world trapped between two suns. Using knowledge and technology turning the planet into an inter-universal starship the Nibiru without the fuel to run it. The fuel being the DNA of a human Michael. The scientists sacrificing their own material to ignite the machine. In the end Michael would be manipulated by Nergal into entering a DNA extraction machine.

Michael, the modern human sent back in time by the mysterious old man after meeting Vorigon, The Man in Black, face to face on Dyaus. Only to be sent to an unknown period of the Earths historical past. Michael is stranded on a fifth planet Tiamat to find it is covered in bio-domes filled with genetic mutations by the Nephilim seeking to obtain material. The planet Gia was being terra-formed by the Nephilim using the trees, wildlife and soil from Tiamat. Gia, having been destroyed in a cataclysmic collision between the Nephilim when the Nibiru drifted out of control.

The Nephilim seeing a world covered in a forest seeking to find that specific point in space time where the manipulation of DNA would produce a human. Humans being the perfect manifestation of the source in this reality. Only isolated points in the universe create humans. In the process saving the Carian from the dying Venus and burning Earth to the planet Mars. The Nephilim give Seraphim several Ahtna monkey from Tiamat to use for genetic research. The Seraphim, masters of DNA manipulation were saved only out of respect to their advanced genetic engineering abilities. The Seraphim are even better at genetic engineering than the Nephilim, which is why they are fed material little by little to prevent them from leaving the surface of Mars. The Seraphim living under the surface of Mars due to the atmospheric differences.

The Seraphim were required to provide gold to the Nephilim in order to receive more genetic material. The Reptilian Seraphim created advanced primates from the DNA of the Ahtna of Tiamat to mine the needed minerals and live on the surface of Mars.

The quantity of gold mined not sufficient to return the Nephilim to the Nibiru trapped in orbit around the dark star. The advanced primate becomes an independent being living on the surface of Simud. Simud is covered in oceans with savannah marshlands dominating the surface. The people of Ares genetically advanced by the Nephilim begin to develop interpersonal relationships and autonomous thought. Beginning the steps towards independence. The existence of a being resembling a human catches the eyes of the Nephilim.

The Nephilim realize that Earth is the location in space time where genetic manipulation would create a vessel which would provide the genetic material needed to power the Nibiru. In order to provide Nergal with the tools to achieve his freedom the Nephilim require Nergal remain on the Nibiru until it is powered on and brought back to Gia. Once at Gia the Nephilim plan to kill Nergal. Nergal wise to the deception of the Nephilim begins using the power of the Nibiru to build a massive army of Grays organic machine replica's using the DNA of the Nephilim Greys. The Nephilim greys are the genetically engineered helpers of Mastema and his scientists who cover the surface of Tiamat. They prepare to release a second wave of capsules towards the Earth.

The true history of a moment in time for universe of origin is explained. A big bang occurs when two universe collide. Every universe is contained within a bubble floating in a river called the source. The source is a self-aware consciousness that watches over all lifeforms within the game. The consciousness of the source moves like honey surrounding and protecting the infinite universal bubbles contained within its liquid. The liquid of the source is also filled with infinite numbers of consciousness seeking entry into a universal bubble. When the two universes collide one universe consumes the other.

Two particular universes that have completely mastered by their manifested species. The universe of the Carian collides with the universe of the Anasazi. The Anasazi material flows into the universe of Carian expanding the universe destroying the culture of the Empire of Carian. The Native Anasazi descended from the Tanye Tanka who resemble sasquatch were giant ancient natives themselves.

The leader of the Anasazi is Kulkukan who resembles the image of the source when appearing to Michael. Kulkukan is an eternal being who always makes big picture decisions viewing the entire scope of the river of life and the role of the universe(s) within it.

The Nibiru is hijacked by Nergal who seeks to sabotage the Nephilim plans is undermined when Michael and Ares detonate the planet Tiamat. The explosion destroying the fifth planet Tiamat leaving the Nibiru inoperable. The destruction blasts the atmosphere and oceans off Mars towards the planet Earth with many large icebergs becoming trapped in the Earth's orbit. Earth is covered in bio domes previously released by the Nephilim from Tiamat to flood the planet with genetic creations in preparation for relocation. With the destruction of Nibiru, the Nephilim are in disarray trapped on the world. The interdimensional hopes crushed as they became isolated. The Earth is covered in large buildings place together in geometric slabs of stone. The Titans dominate the surface of the planet. Created by the Nephilim using human DNA and Nephilim DNA were merciless. Titans are tall with translucent white skin with black eyes. They control the advanced primates who are mining for Gold.

Ares, the leader of the advanced primate's searches for his family who have vanished from Mars. The formerly loyal body guard military commander for Nergal. Now making decisions for the future of his own people aligns himself with Michael, a human from the future who Ares aspires to be. Michael, viewing Ares with respect as an autonomous equal. Michael encourages his ability to make independent thoughts and decisions for himself and his people removing the illusion of Gods, revealing the Seraphim of Nergal as Tim Gods. Ares and his people are freed from oppression.

It is revealed that Ares is a human of Mars. In the universe of origin location plays a factor in genetic engineering. One degree to the right of Earth the creation of Ares. One degree to the left of Earth the creation of Nergal. The vessels having different manifestations but the consciousness equal and from the same location. The perfect vessel for genetic engineering for the eternal consciousness found on the Earth.

There are those from outside the river of life which contains the bubbles of universes that watch. These beings acting as watchers are tall with white skin and unlimited power. Michael calls them the Tall White's. The Tall Whites are unwilling to dramatically alter the timeline. Appearing at sporadic but rare moments in human history to help humanity's progression towards becoming advanced humans. Michael realizes advanced humans live in a realm called Origin. An alternate realm that existed separate from the source and the universal bubble. The understanding of the machine that holds all within bound expanding.

Michael overcomes an encounter with Vorigon, a being from a realm of darkness that is not fully understood. The man in black unknown in origin with no details how his story unfolds. Being sent to the past Michael seeks to prevent the future events from happening all-together. After an initial battle of back and forth questioning whether he was delusional or not, choosing to believe he was in Earth's past. Michael brings about a leveling of the playing field at the direction of Kulkukan, with the destruction of Tiamat, Nibiru, and Mars as habitable destinations. He is faced with the reality that all creations would be confined to the planet Earth. Itself hemorrhaging slowly back to life.

Nergal the genius species from Venus. The former rulers of the universe. The driven serpent seeking to utilize the knowledge of the future of the planet begins again in Antarctica. Seeking an uninhabitable location, the hundreds of thousands of Gray's build massive underground bases. Nergal, carrying his insurance policy, his guarantee within eight clones of Michael who he calls the Illuminati. The Illuminati are advanced seraphim reptilians. The plan of last resort which he feels is full proof. Eight human clones of Michael genetically engineered using Seraphim (reptilian) DNA. Raising the creations from cryogenic stasis Nergal announces them as eternal beings who would be founders of a future empire as the Illuminati. The founding fathers and mothers of the organization that would infiltrate the human world for manipulation and the benefit of the Nergal's vision to conquer the planet and use Earth as a base to reclaim the universe. Nergal names his Illuminati. The advanced humanoids are able to shape shift into any creation they touch. He calls them the future of the species, the new children of the Carian. Nergal sends his eight children to the corners of the globe to establish new cultures and civilizations.

Kulkukan flees the planet Tiamat in a Nephilim ship which he buries within a granite mountain. His people, the Anasazi rebuild forming a hidden culture high within the cliffs. The planet Earth has been overrun with massive lizards who covered the post-apocalyptic planet prior to cataclysms of Tiamat and Simud. The stage is set for a new confrontation with Nergal, Michael, Ares, Kulkukan, Mastema and his creations isolated on a blue marble.

2

PHASE II

The decision to destroy the planet took courage and patience but it was accomplished. These were decisions with consequences larger than themselves. Whether justified or unjustified much greater power than one man should have been given. To avoid war is the theme of life unless of course you live in the universe of origin where genetic variation is infinite and king.

In the universe of origin, the governor of the machine is a conscious entity named the source. Within the source infinite universal bubbles projecting the illusion of reality for cloned consciousness to dwell. Illusions of reality, creations of the sub atomic matrix that allow the soul to exist, a separate extension of the source. The source was self-aware viewing all human life as its children with it a good steward. The real question as what was consciousness and why it needed to dwell within vessels. Why were vessels so unique and while all consciousness was equal the vessels could be dramatically unequal.

Michael ran these thoughts through his mind over and over.

The rundown of the timeline far beyond remembering every detail he was lucky to survive. Seeking answers that he could not find. Which seemed just beyond the veil. He had met a superior life form. A sentient being that was self-aware. Not only self-aware but that which built and maintains the framework that he exists within. In all places, at all times. Why this framework and why the need for an overseer and how could he exit?

The source was looking for storytellers to tell a story within the game called life. A speculated simulation replaying a story of some long lost time. Knowledge that none but the source contained. Michael chuckling to himself was getting goofier and goofier the crazier and crazier things got. It just didn't seem real anymore. The depth of his philosophical understanding pressing against the walls of the cranium challenging his mind to unshackle itself.

A mind that natural sought to why. A consciousness that did not originate in the machine. That did not originate within the vessel of his body. Yet he had a vessel that seemed to contained the most powerful genetic elements in this universe. Perhaps this was because he was the manifestation of the source in the perfect location. Michael was forced to take this thought process seriously due to the fact they kept capturing him and sucking him almost to death. Something existed within the cells. Something unseen that formed the fabric of the vessel which he resided within that caused a few interdimensional beings to go at great lengths to obtain. Of course this was the reason why.

The planet was not in full blown civilization over drive as in past moments. All groups were simply trying to survive. Michael marveled at the numerous groups on the surface all striving to be the first to reach space. To reconnect with something that they once lost. Something that was all encompassing, their life, taken in an instant. When knowing everything turns into having nothing but vague memories of something that used to be but no longer was.

Along the equator the civilizations of the Nephilim flourished. The dark creatures led by the indomitable Titans building the foundation for many civilizations that Michael recalled from his lifetime. Their cities made of massive stone to last millennia as monuments to the giants of the planet.

The Seraphim Illuminati began sneaking into these civilizations, infiltrating their governments. The ruling families of Nergal children taking over leadership. Viewed as Gods by the people of the Earth the Nephilim waged a never ending war against the Illuminati. The ability to adapt giving the Illuminati the upper hand in blending in to both other cultures. They were sly and subversive while the Titans were bold and domineering. One was a chameleon while the other was a fifteen foot giant. The odds of assimilation seemed in the favor of the Illuminati.

The reality of the constant conflict was the norm of every single day for Michael. It was his job to find those points in time and remove the potential. Unable to conquer, he could repeat instances such as Tiamat and the Nibiru explosion on a smaller scale. At least in theory. A theory that could not be proven. Michael entered the quarters of Kulkukan.

Kulkukan rising and greeting both Ares and Michael with a huge hug. "You have done it. You have balanced the scales. You have leveled the playing field."

Michael was smiling it was pure happiness to see Kulkukan again. Michael then asked the question he had been dying to ask. "When I was in Tiamat before I merged the crystal with the core. I explored your old room. I found the hand print on the wall. I saw the video. What does this mean? I understand you somehow came here during the big bang when your galaxy merged with this galaxy. But when, how, please tell me so I can understand?"

Kulkukan, recognizing that there existed few moments in life that an individual would be prepared to address the possibility of such answers took a moment. He responded to Michael. There are questions that exist that while seeming simple will challenge the foundation of any being's philosophy. I had found it better not to address such matters as few were worthy to receive them." Kulkukan stopped speaking and began moving his fingers along the beads as he had done in Tiamat. "20 billion Gia (Earth) years ago. My people resided in a realm that was in perfect harmony with itself. Faced with invaders we chose to enter a universal bubble to assist in the destruction of this universal bubble." The revelation shocking and beyond comprehension for Michael. "We were the Anasazi. We filled every world around every sun in every galaxy in that Universal bubble awaiting the moment when we would come. I am the last eternal being of my people here.

Kulkukan was pacing still running his fingers across the beads.

"Long ago, several of the wise elders determined to preserve the history of our ancestors. Our ancestors the most important of our entire culture. A process that changed the DNA of our species to Eternal was performed on myself and several hundred Tanka. They were and are us in the beginning. The ones you see now will live with me forever. My people have not been changed. They will live their lives and return to the source to begin their journey home united with the family of your consciousness. We are being grafted into your eternal family. We became aware long ago that we were surrounded by many other heavens. When the breach occurred we prepared ourselves. The mass of our heavenly sphere twice that of the colliding heavenly sphere. We determined that our mass would burst through into the other sphere. Riding the vastness of space and time is quite simple in scale to size when suns are separated by vast distances. The distance we travelled as the entirety of our universe merged with this expanding and pressing it outwards in compensation to the matter was instant. We survived an event that is unparalleled in the existence of intelligent beings."

Kulkukan looked up at two of the tall native giants grasping one of them by the arm. "The vast majority of my species occupying the seven sisters of the Pleiades Star System. Our elders require a thick forested planet to survive. The world Tiamat was discovered. Covered in forest and ruled by a primitive monkey was the perfect home to start over. My role as eternal leader was to preserve their lives. When we arrived the Carian Empire had collapsed. They were confined to the surface of their world. Polluting the atmosphere trying to escape its surface. Some stranded on Earth and others dying on the moon. We accomplished our task and our realm was preserved."

Pausing to pick up a homemade flute, Kulkukan played a soft tune which caused all the holographic fires to turn on. "I knew then it would take a miracle to save that species from themselves. This species that formerly ruled the entire universe trapped on a planet they could not escape. Determined to escape at the cost of their own annihilation. The decision was paramount to blind suicide. They all knew the truth, but pretended it did not exist. Knowingly agreeing to their own death. My people are old. Many times older than this universe. We will wait it out until it is our time again."

"What about the Nephilim?" Asked Michael.

"They are from a place outside the river of life. Stranded here by as fallen ones. When they appeared it was only a few thousand years ago. Their world was on a collision course with Gia, your Earth. As they entered the solar system they became aware of the habitable worlds with life focusing on Tiamat. Gia was doomed to extinction. Simud only containing large plant eating lizards. The same as covered Gia prior to the collision. When they came to Tiamat they captured and killed so many. The reality of what they were doing to my people the Anasazi, and the Ahtna monkeys was unbearable. The lengths at which a Seraphim will go are beyond acceptable."

"Michael, in every place the creation of a hominid is possible. The end result is never the same. I have told you this over and over but look at this being." The holographic imagery shone a chimpanzee with arms stretched the same as the Vitruvian Man. "This is the human of Tiamat. The Ahtna, the monkey is the result of genetic engineering to create hominids on that world." Michael stood in shock. His theory was correct. The body was merely a vessel. Staring at the giant monkey. A tall chimpanzee the size of a man but very much a giant chimpanzee was only a vessel for consciousness. His theory was proving correct.

"These beings really are you. They are me. They are us, all of us emerging into this existence through the source. To consider oneself superior is foolish indeed. Look at Ares, the hominid of Simud, and look at you, the hominid from this very world. The only difference is that when you were created you happened to be at a spot with a greater connection to the source. The Apex. So you entered the vessel with greater function and ability within this realm of illusion. You could have entered a vessel from Simud. Consciousness is equal and the same. Gia is a remarkable planet. The only we have found in this entire Universe that produces a vessel such as yours. In every universe while infinite worlds are projected with consciousness only one is an apex that produces the perfect vessel but they are only vessels. No vessel should be leveraged against any other. What you have shown with Ares is that those created one degree off can develop greater ability over their vessel through individual choice when given access to information."

Kulkukan turning the screen to show the Pleiades Star System. "My people are coming. With the core of the world in detonation a signal should have been sent to them. The time has come to infiltrate one of the Titan stronghold cities. If Ares people are to be saved. We very well cannot walk out with them."

"I can't allow them to stay there under those conditions, Ares won't allow it" Michael said directly as he was already preparing to leave. "I think we take over a city. I think we do something that will put them on their heels. The cities are too large to gain access from a frontal assault. I figure we would need to infiltrate into the population. Create an uprising from within." Michael giving his plans showing he had been thinking about this for quite a while. Kulkukan was intrigued.

The holographic image of the Titan temple rising like a towering pyramid. The perfect digital matrix of the nearest fortified city appeared in front of them. The actual building was slated with granite slabs. Smoke steamed through the air around the temple square.

Ares was eager to see what his two friends were doing before pointing to the map and stating, "We must enter from here." Ares pointing to a clusters of trees that extended over the top of the east wall. "How do you know this will be the spot too cross?" Questioned Michael not wanting to challenge him but to ensure it was the right spot.

"I've already been there." Ares revealing his intelligence and ability to keep a secret. Michael looked at Ares with a smile. "While in this place, you must also seek to find Ahtna. It is of great importance we locate any surviving ape species." Kulkukan then issued the directive. "Phase II will be the freeing of Ares people." Sealed with the grasping of each other's forearms in the sign of the triangle the three dispersed. Michael and Ares walking towards the starship once again determined to succeed. They were brothers and neither could imagine not having the other around. Michael was thinking again about his friend Ares. How can anyone understand the dynamic of having a twin brother unless you yourself have had a twin brother? In a reality where humans were interplanetary cousins with all other hominid species in an endless search for greater enlightenment the forces at plan were beyond comprehension.

To sit down pen to paper the scope of the reality dared to be imagined let alone accomplished. Would you not be close to the knowledge of the Great Scientist? Michael and Ares ship exited the mountain lowering into the canopy below.

Lizards streaking through the openings. They were the global species. It had been a long time since he had seen any of the other dinosaurs brought to the planet. It was as if an immediate slaughter of all dinosaurs had occurred over night. The species from Mars incapable of adapting. The carcasses littering the ground. The world would remember them as clusters of carcasses in the geological historical record. As if their entire existence ceased in an instant.

The age of the dinosaur had ceased instantly.

The Tyrannosaurus Rex was terrifying. There were many versions. Tall ones that tower near the canopy of the trees, they were rare, and every other variation down to the size of your hand. The chemical fallout from the collision of the Nibiru causing mighty beings to come into existence. The only safe places on the planet were along the edges of the poles or deep within the Earth.

"We need to land the ship Ares; this has to be done on foot." Michael knew that if they were to actually succeed in infiltrating a city. Flying to the door might be a poor decision.

"Yes, I agree." Ares directed the ship towards a dark corner of the deep forest. Michael pausing to realize this was the first time that Ares had referred to himself in the first person that he believed that Ares believed he was equal. "Ares, let's land over there under that large tree. We can cover it with debris. Although, I am not sure it will really matter."

Landing the ship, the two exited cautiously. Looking through the perimeter always watchful of the frontward charging teeth baring moving muscle of a Titan they were on edge. They stepped through the canopy. The distance one mile from the rising pyramid. The pyramid built near a massive quarry. The ground covered in the most beautiful pine needles. Michael's feet gently sinking into the moist soil. The moss covered trees left a smell in the air that was refreshing and brisk. Crisp air breezing through the valley.

The sounds of drums could be heard beating in the distance. Boom. Boom. Boom. Boom. The beats echoing through the valley. Ares and Michael using them to get close to the high walled city. Making longer sprints when the drum beat was echoed. Ares moving towards the wall with the large tree that he had been using to gain access into the city. With the sun setting the dusk concealing their movements the two began the ascent into the high walled city.

3

NEPHILIM

The Nephilim had been the scourge of the solar system for millions of years. Their emergence to a world covered in monkeys threw an entire universe into chaos. The thought process revealing that this part of the universe had been genetically altered by a prior civilization. A precursor to the Carian.

Someone had to have created the monkeys. The genetically engineered hominids. Mastema was the leader of the Nephilim and none more knowledgeable on genetic engineering. Their journey to the source planet was filled with constant struggles to overcome an eternal punishment.

He was one of the first creations of the Brahma. Given the job of creation. His kinds were geneticists. The realm containing expanding creations.

Through his research with the manipulation of the source which was a literal river flowing through Dharma. Mastema had learned that his creator, the Brahma, was in fact a creation himself. Mastema recognized the possibility of space time variations. Testing this hypothesis in the realm of Dharma. He would need to create a tear in space time to access other dimensions. The temporary simulated universes within the river of life that flowed through his laboratory seemed like the perfect place to initiate his grand experiment.

Isolating the fluid, he began sending out genetic code into the consciousness of the river that when applied within the sub atomic matrix of the river identified habitable locations where consciousness originated. His job was to isolate and extract consciousness from the river to create new Brahma like himself. Emerging with no memory these beings were taught the same as he to do what he has done. Never thinking to look within the spherical units inside the river.

The universe would behave like a hard drive that he would download information to connect the dots back just a bit further. The code was simple, in any location that allows for the implementation of the creation of a hominid fitting certain parameters physiologically. Parameters for life in Dharma. These points were then proven to exist within the spherical units inside the river and not the fluid they had been using to create more of their kind. The source sending out the confirmation to Mastema suggesting that indeed locations existed that allow the perfect manifestation of the source within the simulated matrix, the emergence and creation of an eternal being. This placed everything he did into jeopardy. If this was true, indeed it was, he was prematurely extracting consciousness. If that was true than all Brahma in Dharma were trapped.

Mastema in that moment realizing that the great Brahma was nothing more than his own intelligence. Confronting the Brahma, Mastema began sharing his data. "Great Brahma, I am troubled." "What is it my son?" Responded the Brahma, the leader of the realm of Dharma.

"Since you created me and asked me to be a creator. We have filled this realm with life and always more to bring from the river of life." Mastema was confused and struggled to understand what he had seen.

"Yes, this is true, we bring advanced humans into existence." Brahma responded causing Mastema to pause. "How do you know they are advanced humans? Yet, I am troubled because of something that I have learned. In the river of life, in the sub atomic vessels of souls. I found something. My calculations show there is the possibility of the creation of beings like you and me inside the river at specific points. If this were to be true and that soul was harvested would it not bring into existence another being like you?"

Mastema rising twelve feet in height questioned his leader. While in the process of extracting fluid from a machine to genetically engineer new being he stumbled upon the reality that other realms exist beyond his own. His long flowing garment always waving in the air as his feet never touched the ground. His skin translucent purple. Skin smooth with a soft edge glowing around its perimeter. They were purple humans in a realm of tranquility. The Great Brahma pondering the revelation before responding. "Considering what you are saying is true. I want you to send into the river of life a program instructing it that at no point is there to be a possibility for the creation of a Brahma."

Mastema pausing to realize what he was asking. Mastema realized the liquid was a super computer. It was a code that could be tweaked to do varying things. Within the code an equation existed proving their own existence in relation to the source itself. The program had now proven that Dharma may in fact be just another part of the program. That within the river other beings perhaps more powerful than Brahma may exist. He quietly responded. "Very well."

Leaving his leader, Mastema was shocked at Brahma dismissiveness acknowledging it was true. What would happen if a Brahma were a created being? He had asked him to input the code sequence. He could have done it with the swipe of his hand. He was the Brahma.

Entering his research facility. The clear glass walls emitted perfect light. Moving to the material coding stream a long tube of brightly lit substance carried from the left of the room to the right. In the center of the tube insertion points to inject or extract the substance. Moving to a white keypad Mastema began typing with his six human arms. His fingers moving at such an incredibly rapid rate lines of code written into perfect strips of genetic orders. The material a substance that works as code when submitted into the source implemented into the digital matrix. It was simple. He extracted liquid. He imputed code provided to him by Brahma. The production of another Brahma like Mastema came into being. He was an engineer of Gods.

Pausing in hesitation, Mastema went back to the keypad. Reinserting the small chip with a clear glass capsule on the end into the computer. "Let's mask you a bit. We won't remove you from the matrix, but we will hide your possible locations." What Mastema had done was not eliminate the possibility of the perfect creation, rather he would simply limit its occurrence in a sea of code making it more difficult to recognize."

He knew the stark reality of the implications of his find. For the first time in his existence he was defying his creator. Never before had he considered his creator was a created being. The Brahma, was, well the first Creator. With the possibility that other dimensions existed separate from his own that may look down upon him. The Brahma had been expanding his realm with many creations. Namely the armies of eternal beings that he created from the source which acted like a river in their world.

Their world stretched into infinity in all directions. It was the flat world without end in a realm of pure existence. Mastema began thinking about his leader. The Brahma had the power to manipulate space time in a place of pure matter. He brought the order that makes life possible. This was a harvesting center. Mastema mind was racing, for the first time in his existence he felt a fraud. A foolish pawn in the enslavement of sentient beings. Celestial enslavement.

Turning to the flowing input access point that allowed access into the source. Mastema submitted the coding necessary to ensure that he would not be the one to cease the creation of Brahma within the river. Considering the reality if this were truly possible. Were their other Dharma? Places similar to his own, ruled over by another Brahma. Endless as the Vessels of souls in the river of life. Was he but one of numberless who became aware? Mastema then determined to organize his information to share with others within the High Council of Dharma.

Being the first of any species carried power in the Halls of Immortals. Genetic manipulation in a realm above all others producing super beings. He being one of many within the Brahma leadership council. Looking down within the flowing liquid he could see small bubbles of encapsulated universes. The filaments of atomic matter stretching to hold the universe intact. The life that must exist. The beings existing in these places that are seeking to obtain transcendence to Dharma or was he transcending to that place. Must he descend beneath it all to make things right entering the microcosm of a reality that he could destroy with a press of his thumb.

The process of bringing souls of humans to Dharma producing

the birth of immortal men and women with memories of their past lives was his greatest honor. Mastema relished his role as leader of the process. A process that the Brahma had shown to him. In the coming moments upon the world of Dharma. Mastema had assembled a team of like-minded concerned followers. The implications, if true, demanded the immediate liberation from the control of this powerful being, who was not one and all, but one of many. Who had tricked them when they had thought they had escaped the cycler of souls only to realize they had not even begun.

The structure of creation for Mastema expanded in this moment, he could see within universes souls bursting into existence. Moving from the fluid into the spheres. Not from the fluid into Dharma. The system showed that only by entering a sphere would a soul transcend the river of life to emerge at a Dharma naturally. Yet the sequence of numbers said if this were true than only one could emerge naturally within any given realm while all others would be subject to entering the sphere. Meaning, only through outside manipulation would a realm like Dharma become filled with immortal beings. It was backwards and showed that Brahma had done something wrong turning Dharma into a soul harvesting facility. Ruled by a Brahma, the all-powerful God. But with infinite Brahma, each with their own Dharma ruling within a larger cosmology. Who then created the Brahma?

Mastema eternal mind bent with questions that reached for answers just beyond his grasp. Yet, as with the consciousness living in the worlds within the river of life some things even he could not confront with answers from his own mind. What he needed to do was find another Brahma. To reach out and merge the reality of his realm which was cosmic beyond without limitation of size to the realms within the source. Creating an interdimensional rift connecting the two realms equally at one point of transition between the two. But this would only be possible if Dharma was in fact a part of the code.

In this case the process would bring both realms onto an equal playing field in terms of size, the rift compensating for the space time continuum. If he could access one of the universes within the source the possibility existed, he could reverse the process connecting that realm to another Dharma. Perhaps if he could find another Brahma or the creator of all Brahma. He could obtain the answers he so desperately needed but he needed to test his hypothesis first.

It had never occurred to him that in the process of genetically engineering human beings in Dharma that he was a part of the process. While all of these retained memories of their lives in the river of life, none had ever emerged as a Brahma. Most all considered their life a resurrection in an afterlife. Eternal beings entering the Dharma ruled by Brahma. The mathematical possibility proving that at any point a being could emerge with the collective memory of all creations was rare. The manifestation of the consciousness of the river of life, the source, in this world. It would be considered a glitch.

Never before had it occurred to Mastema that the Great Brahma was created. In this moment Mastema, sought to know who brought Brahma to life here? In his world there were only eternal beings engaged in the harvesting of souls from the great river and manipulating material for personal satisfaction and comfort. The agenda of why never shared, only that it must be done to accumulate the most possible beings to expand the kingdom.

Mastema considered, perhaps there was a reasons there was a stress of urgency at all times as if something may or would happen to bring conflict. It was as if Brahma knew he did not control the presence of the source and feared its disappearance.

The cosmological mountains that Mastema was forced with overcoming were at times too much to bear. Not in desire, his heart pressed against his soul to know why? The pressure of reaching for the outer branches of the tree limb made the base of his skull and his cranium feel as though they were stretching under the force of the unseen demanding access to knowledge that he did contain. Willing it to himself from an information highway that completely surrounded him.

The theory was plausible. He would use the genetic manipulator to focus an endless stream of power into a specific location in his world. It would have to be in his laboratory. He would program that stream with a code linking it to a programmed destination of the same stream inputted into the source. In theory he was making several guesses based on his idea Brahma was one of many. The first, he was hypothesizing that he in fact was also part of the matrix. While on a grander scale he too was subject to the digital illusion of reality. If this were true, then it would make the second truth absolute, if his world was in fact a manifestation of the matrix it could be coded, it could be changed.

This code could coincide with another point at any location macro or micro in the sub atomic matrix within the river of life. Meaning, he could appear anywhere at will as long as he was aware and had access. Of course, it was all a hypothesis. He had the skill, the technology but never the thought to try it. If he was wrong, he could create a reverse wrap in the space time of his world. That paradoxical black hole wrapping upon itself possibly destroying them all. The effects would most certainly be catastrophic.

Mastema determined either way to find out where Brahma had come from and perhaps where the Brahma goes when he leaves. The word had begun to spread among the Dharma immortal that they were possibly on a temporary world themselves with access to greater worlds and knowledge. People began to question the Brahma, the comfort of their lives. Why so many of them were required to inhabit this space in an endless expanse, to simply expand? Many always felt there must be something more but accepted the reality of Dharma. Some beginning to question within themselves whether or not Dharma's existed with beings the same as themselves. The idea could not be stopped permeating the people in all areas of Dharma. A realm very much like the worlds they each remembered.

Mastema knew the reality of heaven is only as true as the knowledge of the space to which you go or come. If upon arriving after death it is realized another society exists to which you must conform even in the heavenly realm who would not? If one, then became aware that within this space of eternity there are many kingdoms in the afterlife it opens the door for the possibility that there will exist those with more knowledge of what it all means than yourself. Would not the eternal being in the heavens aware of other heavens seek to use their free agency to leave? What if someone kept you from leaving when you rightfully could, was this not what Brahma was doing? He must find these answers.

Mastema wanted to know. He was not an advanced human being in perfect form. He was not a being who carried the memories of a previous life from within the matrix creation of the source. He was a created being unique to his origin. If he could go to where they came from he could also understand why it is so important that they transcend that micro reality through to appear in this macro reality. The moment of time had arrived, the genetic amplifier focused on the wall of the laboratory. The surface made of the same eternal material present within the landscape. A landscape present before he was created of pure matter with this unknown river of life. What form of creation did he reside? He looked inward as well as outward choosing to accept the impact of the bigger question.

Numbering ten created architects the same as Mastema. What was interesting about them and their position was that none of them retained a memory. Dharma was filled with many who did with Brahma retaining the memory of something else. They were chosen to perform these experiments as geneticists because they retained no memory. Brahma was proving to be the master manipulator. How efficient to place those who would never seek because they did not know to the river that contained all life. Here they were the third of the high council leadership. This was a critical blow to the future of Dharma. They agreed on one thing. They deserved the opportunity to be masters to their own destiny. To see for themselves the outer realms of creation. To obtain the knowledge that they rightfully deserve to know. Driven by an environment of willing suppression Mastema was bothered that Brahma knew something that he would not share. Brahma obtained knowledge that he did not provide any opportunity to obtain. He was the first to ever enter within Dharma.

Was not his individual soul worth as much as all other eternal souls above and below? Placing a tube that connected directly to the access point for the source. Mastema opened the flow to provide the source code into the tube leading to the machine. Taking a large glowing syringe, he inputted the coding which pinpointed the arrival of a specific space in one of the universes. It was all code so finding the number of a specific location superseded depth and perspective. The location near the mathematically predicted apex where a Brahma could be created. The code ensuring a link to a computer simulated destination. Moving to the machine the beam programmed to input the same code into the material that formed the wall of his laboratory. To many of the geneticists in the room it was a ludicrous idea. If correct would have a monumental impact on their reality that they could not accept.

The flow of the glowing source material powering the device. It was something he had never done. He redirected the flowing liquid to pass through the device producing a beam of focused energy. The beam blasted towards the wall. The theory suggesting the wall was the same matrix as within the source meaning everything was a simulation. As the beam beat down upon the wall the surface began glowing a brilliant white. The energy began affecting the source material until it was glowing as well. Looking at the computer to confirm the code accurate Mastema pressed the control to link the two locations the code had linked. Instantly the wall pealing back to reveal an opening ten foot in height and four foot in width. It performed exactly as it was instructed. The room stood silent as all knew every had changed.

Walking towards the opening they all peered in to see what was on the other side. A dark work covered in ice. The frozen wind whipping into the room. They knew. They too were part of the simulation.

Mastema turning to the others. "You see here is what I believe and aim to prove. I believe that Brahma originally appeared here first. I believe in being first he obtained access instantly of all things. He chose to go back and bring more of us forward. Abducting consciousness from the river that flowed into Dharma. Those with memories accepted him as the God. Those without he used to work. Why would they question if they had no memory? Why would we question? It is clear to me Brahma has been deceiving us. Either willfully, maliciously or for reasons that he himself does not know we will find answers. Even if those answers reveal Brahma to know nothing. I believe that he knows much more than that."

The next step would be to enter the micro matrix and find the apex where the Brahma would be created. It was Mastema goal to bring the equipment necessary to repeat the process on the micro-matrix level to reveal a conduit to a macro-matrix where another Brahma may exist.

Entering the rift, the breach in space and time the ten beings understood that they were taking the risk of being permanently trapped within the matrix. They also understood that their perspective on death would be different than any life forms they would encounter. The assimilation of life into genetic material would have no eternal significance since their perspective contained the reality Dharma's existed.

Turning to his fellow architects Mastema imparted some words of wisdom. "We will be as Gods, always remember how that feels. To be a God. When we return to Dharma and confront Brahma. We make a pact together. No matter the outcome we will continue forward until we find the source of the Brahma. Will you make this pact with me?" Mastema knew that in a realm of Gods all were equal. The power could not be leveraged. In a realm where there were mortals and immortals leverage could exist. He wanted to know why things are the way they are and always been.

One by one they all agreed swearing an oath against the high council of Dharma and their God leader Brahma. Their only mission in existence to find the creator of their creator. If they couldn't accomplish this task they would be destroyed. If they could they may find salvation. The being that could provide them with the answer to one question, why? Mastema and his scientists were willing to sacrifice their eternal inheritance to enter the mortal realm within the source. Willing to defy their own hierarchy to answer the only question that mattered. Why was it there?

Mastema stood at the gateway with his scientists prepared to make the ultimate sacrifice. Whether for good or for evil it was for all of creation. "Shiva, Vishnu, Ganesha, Kartikeya, Durga, Harihara, Kali, Saraswati, Lakshmi, and Parvati, let us go down among the children of men in their intellectual infancy and let us find the source of the program."

Mastema sealing the doors to the entrance of his laboratory. He would need to leave the machine running in order to return. He hadn't take the time for remote access. He would need the beam intact to return. The beam having its own specific address and location within the matrix. Mastema could access this matrix from any location with his equipment. Without his equipment the knowledge was worthless.

The plan made perfect sense to Mastema, obtain information and return. For eternal beings few obstacles seemed possible within the matrix. Entering through the portal onto the surface of the world the air was a vacuum of electromagnetic energy. They did not breathe air as immortals. This one advantage gave them tremendous leverage within where many were confined to locations based on a program that required them to breath the air of that location to survive. The code trapping consciousness to specific locations for a reason, the program was not what truly mattered. It then crossed Mastema mind, if any being from the Dharma returned into this reality having access to the micro-matrix they could return at any time as an all-powerful God. The power if manipulated into the wrong hands would be catastrophic. He was a code breaker on a cosmic scale. He knew it and hoped that something was watching his manipulation of the source. Brahma had corrupted of the natural chain of life with Gods taken prematurely. A worst Dharma would be one filled with rulers accessing the matrix. He must guard this information. If it were released many would reentering their previous existences to rule amongst the unknowing species.

There was more to the issue here than to find a Brahma, it was to find out why things were the way they are and always will be. The new world was different in many ways. The skies dark with trillions of constellations lighting their view. The purple beings with flowing energy emanating from their backs again stood silent. They were almost angelic in this world.

"Parvati, I would like you to analyze the material that forms the rocks on this surface. See if you can locate any biological material that we can manipulate." Mastema was wasting no time. If time was relative.

Wearing a red colored dress Parvati moved in a majestic feminine way. A female architect was a master of elements. In Brahma using its material to organize fascinating creations. Moving into the distance she began scanning the surface of the stones with a device emitting a blue light onto the ground.

Mastema turning his attention towards the other beings. "Ganesha, you will record everything we do, everything we see, with a specific focus on research analysis." Ganesha, the purple being with six arms like Mastema, however the head of an elephant. He was the recorder of the book of lives in the Dharma.

The other beings were setting up the equipment to begin their experiments. Their six arms moving in ambidextrous ways analyzing the elements. After days of searching the material on the surface of the planet the eleven deities convened to discuss their findings. Harihara speaking up first. "The material of this world is of organic base. If we bio-engineer anything from here it will not produce a Brahma or a being like us. We must move to another location."

Kali looking at Harihara responded with an idea that she had. "We can manipulate the minerals in the ore to build traveling devices. The travel would be slow but we can cross greater distance more efficiently."

Mastema seeing the larger problem had the solution. "Let us

go back to the Dharma. Return tomorrow and try a new location within the radius of the apex. I will fine tune the code to narrow the location of such a world. We can repeat this process over and over until we find the location." Mastema knew that within this spherical bubble there were laws. Al worlds spherical in nature. Programs that grab consciousness and cling them too them. On one such world the children of men would exist. The place of the stories of the memories of those who could remember in Dharma. This was where the answers would lie. On this world the key would exist to help him know why.

The interdimensional generator powering on with a portal opening up a rift. The scientists finishing their research returning to their home world in the macro matrix. Turning off his machine Mastema stood among the others in collective awe. They had done something no other had done. They were pressing forward with something greater than themselves. Something with ramifications they just could not foresee. Mastema was staying up late working on greater mathematical calculations in the area of the universe bubble he had isolated where the apex would be located. He must get closer. The distance in this matrix while smaller than the point of a needle within the micro matrix could be hundreds of light years away. Either calibrate the machine to narrow in on the exact coordinates or spend eternity searching for one location.

To give them the chance of reaching their research goals they must get closer and account for mathematical equations for worlds that are likely to sustain life. Mastema sought rather than shoot them randomly in a specific location he could press further with an algorithm expanding the area to account for planets, stars within the apex.

Leaving his laboratory, he knew that he could not avoid the Brahma. He was the lead geneticist and was required to give an account on numbers of souls harvested as well as their recorded recollections of their lives within the source. Entering the high tower that marked the Brahma's sacred chamber. Crawling on his knees through the doors that led to the entrance. The ceiling of the entrances demanding that all who enter come on knee. The Brahma sat on his throne. The only being in this reality capable of flight. He could instantly create anything, do anything, control anything. He was alone in his power. Who did he answer too?

Rising from the small entrance he spoke the mandatory words. "Brahma, your servant Mastema has come to inform you it is finished. The coding has been entered into the great river. The source will now eliminate within its program the possibility of the singularity apex which would allow for a Brahma to come into creation."

The Brahma peering down through furrowed brow looking suspicious. A look Mastema had never before seen. "Very well my son. What are the current numbers?" Mastema pulling out his keypad. "Three million two hundred souls in the past cycle. The river continues to flow at consistent rates. Should those rates change I will inform your highness." Brahma replying, "Very well. Leave my presence."

Mastema lowering back towards his knees. Crawling back through the entrance into the courtyard. He began to think about his own reality. He too had to process his shift in knowledge. Conform it to all that he knew and using what existed in his own database of knowledge. It was all an effort trying to comprehend those things that seemed too good to be true and yet made a lot of sense.

Why was Brahma always concerned as long as he could remember with the flow of the river and the number of micro-universes per unit? In as long as he had remembered, perhaps an eternity it had never changed. Yet, the Brahma's questioning always implied that it could.

He imagined how his world would respond if the river ceased to exist. It would mean no more souls born into existence. It would mean what? He didn't think anyone would know what to do or where to go. The river itself was a mystery to him. It appeared out of the surface of a stone. Stones in Dharma were made of pure energy. The river coming from somewhere into his existence. No understanding or explanation as to how it got there or how Brahma knew the genetic engineering process was ever shared. Why human beings, why the collection, why the constant need to know numbers? Was there a higher force that kept track to which Brahma was accountable? If there was, Mastema was not privy to this knowledge.

Heading back to his laboratory Mastema began making the necessary adjustments to reenter the matrix of the source. Fine tuning his machine to press further towards the gem. Speaking aloud Mastema processed the moment. "If I am a member of this matrix on a macro level. Where do I go when I die? How do I transition?" The mumbling stopped and he continued to work. At this point never considering that while he brought souls, conscious intelligence from the reality of the micro-matrix into the reality of the macro matrix, why was there no death in Dharma? Dharma was turning out to be a prison and not a salvation. These are fundamentally important questions to ask if it was true. Mastema resolved to press further towards the answers.

Before Mastema had realized his high council returned. Each eager to learn more wanting reentry into the matrix. "I have figured a way to provide a more precise destination. This will continue every time we enter the matrix until we find the place we need. The program implemented will automatically adjust after each trip. The calibration locating more worlds within a smaller radius which meet our parameters. This means eventually we will find the location. We will find another Brahma."

The machine powering back on utilizing the energy of the source to power the beam which opened another door. The group moving to the doorway. A world covered in tall purple stalks and vegetation. The sound of repeated short noises filled the air. A small creature hopped through the door into the laboratory. Mastema picked up the small creature. The larger hind legs, wide mouth, black eyes, slippery skin. He placed the creature back within its own ecosystem. Stepping into the foreign unknown world the air was thick and sticky. The skies colored deep grey overcast. It was the first time that Mastema had ever seen clouds. The first time he had seen material that formed these plants.

With each geneticist moving in their own direction analyzing data. Breaking off pieces of plants, collecting small insects that covered the ground they were taking specimens to analyze. This was a world with life.

Kali, a female geneticist from Dharma walking towards Mastema and Saraswati who were setting up the machines necessary to begin the genetic mutation process on this world. They were setting up a laboratory to begin experiments. "Mastema, I have located the genetic material of a creature with cellular material." Mastema realizing the only true faith is genetic science froze. "Where is it?" Mastema was eager to test this creature first. Holding up the small frog skinned creature with a large head and black eyes he realized it was the same creature that had hopped into Dharma. It was the being that lived in the tree stalks and that ate the insects. It ruled the planet. Was this is the pinnacle species of this planet? He would soon find out.

Mastema excited in delight held the small being in his hands as all stared knowing this was the beginning of something big. Mastema spoke aloud, "Imagination is the beginning of creation. You imagine what you desire, you will what you imagine and at last you create what you will." Placing the small creature into the machine they began the process of extracting its genetic material. One step closer to finding another Brahma.

The process would not harm the creature. Their technique took so little genetic material from each cell leaving the creature without any side effects. Of course they contained the technology to destroy the creature by extracting 100% of the DNA from every cell but they were not killers. The material processing through the machine confirming the elements necessary to produce a humanoid. Whether this was the spot was unknown to Mastema. They could only try the Dharma cloning process and see what emerges.

"We must return to Dharma bring back more equipment. We need stasis chambers. I need to see if this material will create the being we desire." They were trying to create a Brahma. The council returned back to Dharma.

Mastema began wondering if it was better to use source material from his own world mixing the two or should he simply manipulate the DNA of the creature alone. He must try both. He would need to take material with him regardless as they would need more source material to activate the portal to return back to Dharma. All of his equipment utilized the material as a fuel. Mastema began thinking about his own world. Dharma used the source for everything. It was their fuel for the entire society. He considered for the first time that perhaps his life forms in Dharma were acting as parasites entrapping another living organism. The source was not intended to be stripped of its very life. They were guilty of manipulating it for their own progression. He wondered if Dharma was simply a micro matrix of a much larger macro-matrix. Did beings there also use other beings as fuel, as the steps on which to build an empire?

Walking through the towering structures that covered his reality he realized that the very fabric of his society's entire existence was based upon the presence of and the manipulation of the river. Brahma was terrified of the river vanishing. It would mean the loss of the material needed to build and the collapse of their entire civilization.

Mastema knew he was close to something. He could feel destiny calling him, the need for an awakening, the need to open the eyes of the blind to the reality of what exists all around them. In the world of Dharma, days were marked by cycles. One cycle equal to the ring of the bell contained in the tower of Brahma. Which called for all to turn attention to their creator and devote all actions to him.

After the end of the day Mastema again arrived at his laboratory. His processing plant. His access point to the source. His room to view the river which contained the spheres of a digital micro matrix where souls lived lifetimes before being harvested to live in the Dharma. Waiting for the others to appear Mastema noticed it had taken longer for them to arrive than the previous three cycles. Continuing to fine tune his instruments he decided to enter the world alone. He would take the time moving several needed machines prior to the arrival of his scientific team. Back and forth he moved the equipment necessary to clone. As he was coming through the portal from that world he saw a sight that dropped him to the floor.

The Brahma standing amongst his group of scientists. His scientists all on their knees with Brahma's personal guard pressing them down at the neck. Prior to this point Mastema had never seen Brahma or his personal guard ever display aggressive behavior. Though demanding, Brahma was a benevolent and caring creature. This act of violence towards his friends was an unknown concept that troubled Mastema in his heart and mind.

"Brahma, my Lord. I apologize for my unawareness you had entered my laboratory" The angry leader yelling at the top of his immortal lungs. "What have you done? You have accessed that which you were not given stewardship. You have obtained knowledge that was not yours to obtain. You have defiled the spirit of Dharma. You have placed your Brahma in a difficult position. How do I allow you to assimilate back into the Dharma with the knowledge that you now possess? Too do so would be to thrust an entire culture into chaos. Look around you, we have structure, order, and all exist in happiness and peace."

Mastema interrupting the Brahma, "What is the point of existence if knowledge is denied? If the progression of the soul is damned? What purpose is there for any being with no hope that there is more, can be more?"

"Silence creation!" The maleficent being yelled as the vibrations echoed through the walls causing the ground to shake. "Before me was nothing, after me will be nothing. I am the Brahma, the only Brahma, and you are mine. Because of your transgression you and your council are hereby banished to the micro-matrix. To the world of your choosing without access to the river of life ever again. I know the only substance that could bring you back to Dharma so within a sphere I will place you. In time, I will revisit your sentence. My decision is final. Guards, send them through the portal into the micro matrix. I created knowledge and I created the source of universes. Your blasphemy will be removed from the timeline of creation."

Mastema fellow geneticist beginning to weep and sob, begging their Creator to extend them mercy. To allow them another opportunity. Brahma reply harsh and uncaring. "Children, you will have no mercy. Some knowledge must always remain hidden."

One by one the immortal beings moving through the portal onto the surface of the planet. Mastema staring back at Brahma. He spoke a final dialogue to the being. "You are a fraud. Not the only Brahma. Your fear will only grow because you know that I know you're not alone. You are a fraud." Brahma was speechless replying nothing as the portal closing all realizing they were now indefinitely trapped on the surface at the mercy of Brahma.

"How could you let this happen?" Saraswati hysterically crying started wailing on Mastema. The others each with hand in head contemplating their reality. Mastema could see what was happening. "Nothing changes! Any of you think he knows how to use that equipment? He does not know the specific code for this locations address. Look around you, it is all here. I brought it all every piece of equipment that was there. Today was a big day. In fact, if anything has changed it is an increased emphasis on obtaining a gateway to another Dharma and finding another Brahma. We have no other option but to press forward, to find the human specimen we are looking. The work begins now."

Mastema began connecting chords and moving equipment into position. "We knew there would be risks. We knew the answers we needed to find would be found through entering into a simulated universe within the source. It is here the answers are to be found. We are where we need to be to make the greatest impact. We can sit here for eternity until Brahma decides our fate, or we can choose our own fate. Remember upon the conduct of each depends the fate of all."

The eternal beings holding their hands together in a circle with their six arms conjoining forming a wheel. Hands clasped, standing together, Mastema spoke again, "From this moment in time, we will stand resolute to the end. We will be seekers of knowledge. Together." Embracing each other with hugs they gained strength in the presence of another.

Moving towards their machines they began the process of DNA manipulation of the small species on the planet. None spoke but all acted. The cryogenic stasis chamber displayed the structural engineering of the skeletal framework for a body that normally is grown in Dharma. The blood vessels, the capillaries, and the organs all forming within the structure designed to use material to form a humanoid life.

"Lakshmi, I need you to survey the planet for the material called Gold. It will have these calculations of elements. Enter these numbers into your device. Take Parvati, go to the large mountains and begin the extraction process removing, collecting and bringing to me the gold from this planet. It's everywhere. Without access to Dharma, or the source material we must use the closest element to the source which is this Gold. I will finish the creation process of this humanoid to provide you with workers to mine more gold. If this planet is not the apex point of creation, we will need to relocate." Mastema was focused and determined to answer his question, why?

As Lakshmi and Parvati left to find locations where gold would be present Mastema and the other scientists continued setting up the stasis chambers. Mastema connecting the final tube turned the machine on. The streaming canisters of material brought from Dharma lighting the stasis chamber. The fluid flowing into the skeletal frame. Mastema holding a small from in a canister. Injecting the dna of the creature into the fluid from Dharma. Instead of a perfect human being as was always produced in Dharma, laying in stasis was a large seven-foot-tall insect creature. The large bulbous head dominated by massive black eyes. The creature was a humanoid version of the species on the planet mixed with the material of Dharma.

Mastema had in essence genetically engineered life with a conscious intelligence destined to develop self-awareness. This planets version of a human being with a soul. He had successfully pulled a consciousness from the source into the sphere. He was actually helping the process that was previously in play. He wanted to finish his hypothesis. Moving to another stasis chamber he did not fill it with any material of Dharma. This stasis chamber would be filled only with the material of the small creature. Turning the system on the chamber filled with the liquid. Coming to a stop the being in the chamber was a humanoid grey. Wrinkled skin, large eyes, with two arms and legs. "This is not the right location, however let's make more of these to be our workers in this place."

In the process of several planetary months the scientists from Dharma were pumping out endless numbers of these creations. The tall beings unable to speak verbally but with the brainpower of supreme intelligence. As they assembled themselves Mastema explaining that they were their own sentient beings. Brought forth from the source into the micro matrix to assist in finding the location of the Brahma's creation. Mastema explained to them that when they perish here they would live again in another realm called the macro matrix, Dharma as a Brahma.

The genius of the greys was in organizing atoms. The material of the sphere. They began making vessels to travel through space. Mastema realized that with the power that these beings contained. These humans created in a place in space that distorted the version of their existence provided lopsided strengths. They had the power to manipulate elements. Even now they were turning an entire planet into a machine.

Mastema felt with time on his side the best way to traverse space and time would be to do so on a planetary vessel. The main efforts changed from smaller vessels to the ultimate one. Looking at Lakshmi he proclaimed, "This world I call Nibiru. It is the star in the darkness that will find the source of the light."

The focus for Mastema team was to build more Grey's. The advanced lifeforms from this planet, Nibiru. That formula would serve the higher agenda. In time the planet Nibiru rising as a technological machine. The Grey species growing in numbers which increased the rate of production. The humans of Nibiru solely focused on working to assist their creators.

In one of the meetings among the members of the outcast high council the planetary ship was announced completed. "My brethren in this journey. The only dilemma we now face how to power the ship. There is not enough gold in the planet to provide the energy required to power the massive machine. The energy once supplied will course through the conduits of exoskeleton produced by the greys. They are loyal to their home which is now the most powerful home in this universe." He paced through the corridor where the leaders sat quietly staring at him. They had completed the task. None had questioned what they would do once it was completed. How did you start the machine?

Mastem continued to press forward. The machine was based upon the utilization of the source, the material manifested by the river of life within this micro matrix. Mastema had to find a substitute, the material would only be available if he found a human from the apex. Otherwise there was no way to power the ship.

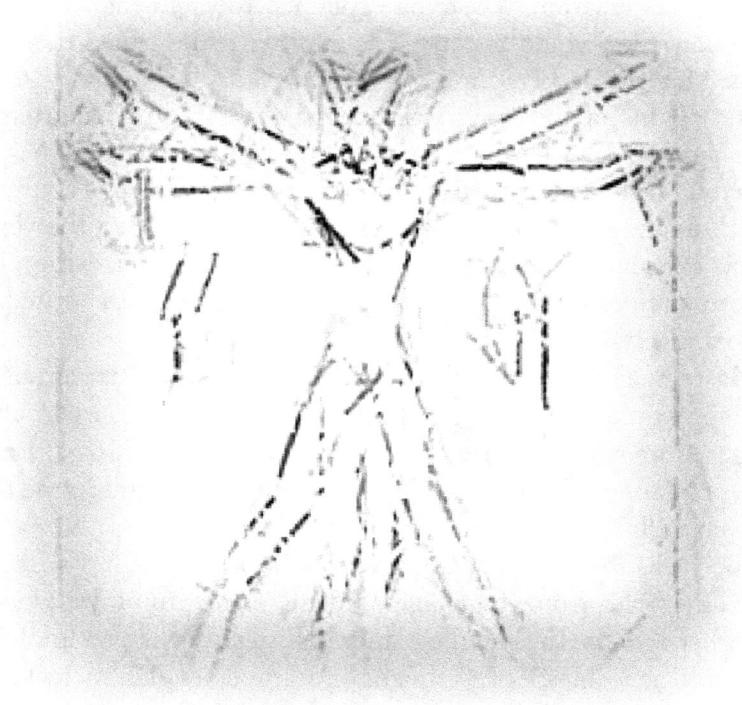

The Goddess Kali stood and walked to Mastema. Grasping a small vile within her hands she turned to the entire council. "There is a way to power this ship. We are eternal beings created from material within Dharma. In every cell that forms us is this source. If we agree to undergo the process of extracting our genetic material, surely then we would have enough material to power the ship. After all, we need but a few drops of source material, do we not?"

Mastema pondered such an idea. Utilizing their own genetic material to bridge the gap. How would it respond, how would they respond physically?

Harihara then stated, "There is a oneness in all existence. I have found with the research of this realm that all things work together to form a greater good. I will go first and perform this process. I will become one with this existence."

Moving into the extraction machine Harihara closed her eyes and awaited the process. The machine pulling at the DNA within her makeup. The material flowing into small glass containers which pumped into a stasis chamber which served as a fuel tank to the entire planet. Falling forward Harihara had sacrificed a portion of herself. An immortal in this reality to the benefit of the mission. He had pushed too far and she suffered much. "All time will remember your sacrifice Harihara. You giving of yourself, half of yourself, for the benefit of all creation. The first of The Celestials to ever subject themselves to such a process."

The being physically ill carried by her kind to rest. Her color faded lighter as if her very essence had been taken. Mastema marveled that such a thing could occur, such a small process, less than what had been done to the small creature. Yet the impact on Harihara changing her color in a way he suspected taking from her life force. Upon further review Mastema realized that without source material Harihara would not recover. He had not considered that eternal being's DNA would not reconstitute or regenerate. The bane of the entire mission. This was only a process afforded to the life forms presence in this matrix who regenerated. Here is was immortal with mortal cellular regeneration while all life within the universe would be mortal with immortal cellular regeneration. In that moment Mastema realized that while a part of the matrix he was also something different and that there was no going back without drastic side effects to include removal of an eternal being from existence.

It was one thing to know for a certainty that all life forms within this universe would live again in a macro matrix. It was another thing to face mortality as a macro being without any knowledge of an afterlife for yourself. If they were to continue the extraction of more material, they would be paying an eternal price. A price that would be reversed once they found the exact apex to produce the Brahma human being. Mastema knowing in that moment each one of them would have to enter the machine, each giving of their life force. Each risking extinction with no way to regenerate material unless they found the apex. An apex they did not have an exact pin point location. A location that may require more material that would require the sacrifice of Gods. They all knew there was no other way.

Mastema moving to the main insertion for the planet. Just a few drops would be enough to power the machine. The duration of powering was the problem. How many drops to power the machine for a day or a week? Connecting one vile of the material extracted from Harihara the machine would insert a drop and then monitor the power fluctuation adding more drops to sustain the planets movement. He knew in the beginning much would be used but as momentum would be gained he also believed he could shut the machine off for longer periods of time. The glowing purple material streaking through the metal framework. Stretched particle by particle. In only one drop of their dna enough material to wrap around an entire planet when extended atom by atom. The planet Nibiru began glowing with red mist being pumped out by the machines moving the engineering liquid. As the material coursed its way along the latitude and longitude corridors the planet jolted with earthquakes. A shaking motion that told Mastema the planet was now moving.

Obtaining his master tablet Mastema could input coordinates in any direction where the probability of the human anomaly may exist. The planet began the process of heading towards an adjacent star system. A star system which was shown to have two stars, one brilliantly lit, the other a red dwarf.

Standing in the main research chamber Mastema showed Durga their destination. "Somewhere in this location I believe is the apex where our research must continue. We will find material somewhere in here that will produce something remarkable. You will see." Mastema programming the massive planet to move towards the star system. "We will need to prepare our long range interceptors to send out drones of the Grey humans. If the world exists we will find planets with life. The closer to the apex the more numerous planets with life. Look for locations with life that is in clusters of planets."

To Mastema is was simple, if a point existed that would produce a God being. It would be surrounded by worlds teaming with life. The residual indication that they were near a creator. Mastema felt so close to finding what he had been searching. He had made the ultimate sacrifice to obtain the truth. Nothing would stop him now. Realized for the first time the single greatest truth. In all known realms of existence in the micro or macro universes he knew as much as the Brahma. At least he knew that much for sure. He was also worthy.

The massive ship grinding to a halt. Mastema running towards the command center as the other architects stood watching as the massive planet drifted towards the distant stars. To his shock the vials of material from Harihara were empty.

"We must reenter the DNA collector!" Durga cried out knowing that one of them would need to make that sacrifice. With none of the architects present Mastema pushes Durga into the machine. Trapping his friend in the sequencing process the machines powers on and then off. The doors open with Durga falling to the ground with the same light blue skin. Transparent and faded Durga was in weakened state. The being giving a portion of its existence, a macro creation interacting with the micro world, it was in this world it could perish. Looking at Mastema the response lacked empathy. "You knew we would all have to undergo the process. Obviously I am last since none know how to run this facility."

Mastema realized the way an advance human being in any macro level could progresses was by coming back to the micro matrix and sacrificing itself to achieve its next step in evolution. Could this be true? Mastema felt the answers to his meaning in life running through his fingertips. They were as close as grasping water. Was he not an advanced being coming back to the micro matrix? He was a being created in another realm, a realm outside of the simulated existence within the river of life called the source. It was in this realm he could have existed for an eternity under the control of a being manifested by the very river. The source was the true harvesters of souls.

The large planet began charging again slowly stabilizing continuing to increase speed. Mastema working constant mathematical equations always seeking to redirect the planet towards the correct grouping of worlds. This was a one shot deal. There were no do overs. They either found the grouping or the long prison sentence towards annihilation by Brahma would begin. One by one the transcendent beings entered the machine. Over and over with continued course corrections. Little by little all beings hanging by a thread to the life they still had waited and watched for salvation and restoration.

As time progressed and the material completely used from each member Mastema himself was forced into the machine. When that material was used the transparent beings inserted themselves again pulling at the very fabric of their eternal existence. They were hovering manifestations of gas losing the density to maintain physical form and unable to suffer death as immortal consciousness from the Dharma. The effort to move things and operate the machine took time but he knew they were close. It had been worth it. The greys now dominating the world. Scouts returning from a distance star system that the Nibiru was drifting. The solar system contained several planets fitting his mathematically requirement to obtain material. His agenda had changed. He needed material to bring form back to his consciousness that hung to a few atoms to keep from being invisible. This was the apex point for his equations. His work, the time, the sacrifice, the giving of his soul.

Alarms sounding the grey humans coming to Mastema informing him that the planet was drifting on a direct collision course with the third planet of the solar system. Fearing death, the architects agreed to give the final collective units needed leaving them hanging barely within this reality and the next. As they entered the machine and the material was extracted, a creature that moved like a ghost flew out of the machine. It was the best they could do. The loss of their genetic material leaving all of them at a fraction of their life force. Still immortal consciousness but without a vessel.

Mastema determined in his mind his death will be in a moment of greatness. In that moment when the truth is revealed after he has sacrificed all of his genetic material atom by atom. When his answers are given and he knows for certain why the Brahma was created and who lies beyond the Brahma? He would live, not die, fighting against the inevitable. Knowing that his sacrifice was all that was needed for his soul to transcend. All this time he thought it was about Brahma, he thought of all the Brahma that may possibly be keeping beings like himself from ever moving on.

The ship was passing through the solar system at an incredible speed. The swarms of grey ships circling the planet like a hive through the air. Mastema stared at the massive red eye looking back at him as the Nephilim soldiers appeared. Imagery shown the coming world to be inhabited with material. The planning was quick, deliberate and efficient. The ancients making the decision to leave the Nibiru. To land on the fifth world covered in a thick forest canopy.

The Nibiru was on a direct collision with the third world with enough force to erase all life or evidence of life from its surface. The cataclysmic collision that would alter all remaining life on the Nibiru as well. The large planet crushing into the side of the Earth. Scraping the crust and stripping material from across its surface before drifting into space out of control in destruction. The planet hemorrhaging with a fracture that wrapped around the world. Only a few places hung on as capable of supporting life. The Earth surrounded by debris as its moon was pelted with melting rock. They became aware they were not alone. Mastema became aware of the remnant of the Carian and the Ahtna monkey.

The grey humans bringing all of the equipment necessary to continue the process on the surface of building humans. The goal, to find the apex returning them to former glory. What all believed was the apex world they had been seeking. Mastema and the other celestial beings believing this may lead to a reanimation of their DNA, a reboot into their system.

Resting in large capsules above the planet. Mastema addressed his ancient scientist who hovered as beings of darkness in the air. "The forest of this world is teaming with life. A very special life that contains material that we can use to rebuild the burning world, reclaim the Nibiru and restore ourselves. You have come so far at such great price. I order the celestial guards to round up every hominid from this world. To strip them in entirety of their genetic material.

Mastema was determined to see these creatures for himself. The shifting entity moving into the transport in a descent to the surface. The team landing, he wanted to see this being for himself. Everything hinged on this moment. Was he in the right spot or did he really need to go to the third world? In the trees movement of creatures shifting in the unseen. The leaves falling from the canopy signifying their presence. Mastema looking over at several grey humans "Go get those creatures, I would like to see them."

The army of Greys pouring into the trees. The commotion and screams echoing through the forest. In a matter of moments, the grey's returning with several six-foot-tall giant humanoid with a long tail and red fur. "A miniature man" responded Mastema. "Run genetic scanning on these creatures. I would like to know if it is naturally occurring or if someone else has been here. I would also like all of their genetic material."

Opening the shuttle doors, the greys drug one of the creatures into the laboratory of Mastema and the scientists. The monkey falling to the ground. Kartikeya grabbing the creature by the chains that bound it dragging it to the DNA extracting machine. The being exiting unaffected by the process. Mastema couldn't believe the being withstood the process. "What do the results say?" questioned Mastema

As they were speaking the ground beneath their feet began to shake. The entire planet wobbling against the impact of the Nibiru and the third planet. "Shock waves" Mastema ordering several of his guards to observe the aftermath for any signs of life. "Research the surrounding planets and report back."

Grey sentinels dispersing from the planet by the tens of thousands. Kartikeya was stunned at what the results suggested. "This is not a naturally occurring creature." She shared the results with Mastema. "What?" responded Mastema confused. "This is being has been engineered on this world. We must be very close to the apex and it looks like someone has also sought these answers." Looking out into the stars Mastema felt the redemption of the moment.

"I want all of their DNA, I want it all, build ships, get us off the ground. We have several worlds to explore." Mastema leaving to cigar shaped ship that transported him from the Nibiru to the surface. In the ship he began reviewing the data returned by the Greys sent out to explore the planets. The results came back quickly with life existing on the second world as well as the fourth world with pockets of remnants of the second world trapped on the third worlds moon and broken surface. Mastema using deductive logic determined. Due to the fact the fifth world is covered in monkeys. The third world is covered in lizards. Both indicated previous explorers seeking an apex. With the fourth world covered in massive plant eating lizards now in a fiery flame it would mean the planet that the Nibiru just annihilated was the apex. How had he destroyed the very world he had been seeking?

The surface was unsustainable for any life let alone a genetically engineered creation. Mastema and his scientists began mixing the genetic material of the lizards from the second world with the genetic material of the monkeys from the fifth. The minor variations still producing enough genetic material to continue researching the differing variations to produce a human being. "We must try endlessly, in any avenue, means or way to produce a human being. This will be the salvation to our kind" The old and decrepit Mastema proclaimed shifting in the air as black mist. Speaking of Tiamat, the fifth word Mastema made a decree. "I want the entire surface of this planet covered in research laboratories. The time for creation has arrived. The moment to seize our lives back has come, we are closer than ever to achieving our goal, to meet the Creator of the Brahma."

The valiant leader proclaimed to beings imparting knowledge and data to their creations. Much of the creating came from the Greys, the genetically engineered hominids of Nibiru. They began the process of stripping the planet of vegetation. Utilizing the material from the fifth planet they became aware that the life forms existing on the second planet faced imminent extinction. A former race that ruled the entire universe until a cataclysmic event destroyed their culture. Mastema marveled at their genetic engineering abilities. They could stretch any material to build anything. He had given them enough material from the fifth world to escape to the fourth world but not enough to allow their abilities to surpass their intellect.

For Mastema, he respected their desire to not accept the reality laid before them and seek to break all the rules in order to answer the questions. He could not in good conscience abandon them on the world to perish when for all intents and purposes they were in the same boat. But he did not trust them, any human variation species that is capable of ruling an entire universe is a foe not to be revered but controlled. Mastema decided the only decision that mattered was giving them what they needed to survive but not enough to provide them with power.

"Send them two monkeys a month." Ordered Mastema to the Greys watching as the Carian species relocated to the fourth planet from the sun. The only place the process would work would be on the third planet, a planet they would need to terra form. The massive machines lifting the trees from the surface, the Greys building transport ships to the third planet, the Cigar Shape moving the large honeycomb sections of the planet to the surface of the third planet.

In time the planet Tiamat was stripped of its forest. During this process Mastema became aware of a being named Kulkukan and his massive hominids. In a desperate effort to capture one they increased the stripping of the planet. The genetic material of its former inhabitants drained. The surface covered in bio-domes filled with life. The beings becoming dark and ominous because of their appearance, the lack of the source within them. Like a withering rose without soil to enrich and water to sustain. The beings fading with time into darkness. The creative process always continuing but the moral compass vanished.

Mastema was nearing a breakthrough in genetic research when he realized that the Seraphim were building hominids on the fourth world. Traveling to the planet he could see villages of miners covering the surface. They had engineered what he could not. What he could do was spray the air with biochemical to advance them even more. He envisioned a world of advanced humans that he could take at any time. Alarmed at the implications he sent for this material using it to being them a bit closer to normal. Instead of mist and transparent the material from the fourth world hominids made them black with form. Using the material, he was also able to increase the pace of the rebuilding of the third planet. Once completed the process could take place restoring them to their former selves, making them something more. Most importantly giving him access to the source to find another Brahma and the answers to the meaning of life.

Mastema considering the possibility with the time to think of what was to come. Finding the apex. An ever moving point in the matrix, this simulated universe. Floating through a river of consciousness. If his hypothesis was correct, there may be an infinite number of Brahma. Consideration for minor to extreme variations of that possible environment the decision to open a window knocking on the door of advanced human beings could have dire consequences. To come this far, the risk did not outweigh the reward, Mastema knew there was no going back. He would see it to the end, his brothers and sisters would as well. Even if it only led to death. He knew that unknown may simply be transcendence to a realm beyond the manipulated relationship of the macro and micro matrixes.

Their Brahma was coming. This he knew. An advanced human who has enslaved an entire resurrected species in an eternal realm. Beings like himself. Mastema drifted deep into thought speaking aloud to himself, "I was born in the Dharma. Therefore, I am the manifestation of the human program in that place. I do not have a memory of my previous life because I had not yet acquired memory within a universal bubble. And yet we share a common matrix, a program, my God only a being born from this river of bubbles with temporary programs of existence could unwind its mysteries." Mastema paused, he knew the answer.

Mastema imagined a Dharma realm that was run by a Brahma that truly was benevolent. A leader that sought to share all of its knowledge, to freely assist in the absolute understanding of why things were the way they are and always have been. How far would he go in this environment to find that being? It was clear that the source was accessible from multiple realms that may not even be aware of each other. This told Mastema that none were the creators of the source any more than a man the creator of a river that provides them with nourishment. But the possibility, mathematically of an absolute realm must exist where there is also access to this same program. He believed a realm existed that brought souls forward from the matrix into immortality and then would proceed to progress that soul with all knowledge.

In the infinite seas of tyrants and dictators, overlords, kings, and queens there must exist one that knows all. A true creator. The puppet master. A great scientist. Had it always been this way? For this purpose, he would sacrifice his own life in the digital matrix where souls are birthed. Mastema pondered the possibility of a macro matrix with a Brahma that only collected Brahma souls. In that extreme environment where all were the same and yet the most powerful beings in the matrix how could a being such as himself even think to survive?

And yet they left an invitation. If he found them would they would view him as inferior, less than? Mastema calling to his Celestials, Karikaya, Ganesha, Parvati, Lakshmi, Saraswati, Durga, Kali, and Harihara as the immortal creations gathered again. Shadows of their former selves nearly lifeless immortal bodies stretched over broken frames shifting between two realities. Their dust trying to blow away in the wind. "We must begin the search for another point in this universe. I have calculated that should the Brahma or whatever leader we find when we open the window into the macro matrix be destructive. To preserve all life in this micro matrix universe, we will also seek to find an opening out of the matrix."

Some of the Celestials words carrying in whispered sentences, "Leaving? Where will we go? How will we survive? Brahma is coming?" Perceiving their weakness in the moment of decision, Mastema was quick to restate his feelings to his friends from the Dharma Realm.

"There was a time when all we knew was splendor and joy. We lived in a place of never-ending joy. Eternal beings. But it came at a cost. The submission to a being, our Brahma. I will have you know now, I know for a fact that our Brahma is one of many. Using the blood of the river of life that flows through his realm to genetically engineer human beings who carry their memories of lives on worlds in the source. Do we have memories? Do we have a remembrance of previous lives? Yet, are we not also manifestations of the source? Ganesha, for the beings inside this simulated bubble the progression is outward. For us, the beings on the outside of the bubble. The ones harvesting souls on the outside of the river of life, this source of information, this intelligent consciousness. The progression is inward. The only way we perish here in this place is with voluntary sacrifice, or at the hands of a Creator."

"Either way, I believe we will face both. I have reconfigured the long range scanners for the locational devices on the ships. They will begin the process of locating the apex to the source of the entire matrix algorithm. I have found a way to isolate the source of this entire source code. What is streaming into the system."

Mastema knew he was smart, and he had always taken pride in his ability to solve complex problems. This was simple mathematics. The entire matrix within this flowing river was digitally simulated matter presenting an illusion of reality. It was a code. To hack into the code, only one from the outside could grasp or fathom the dynamics involved. He was the perfect exception. The scientist responsible for knowing everything there was to know about the strange substance, and the bubbles within it. The possibilities of why the source manifests life forms to experience numberless lives and then reabsorbs them were endless. He had questions like why when he would genetically engineer a human being using this substance it would create an advanced human being, immortal, eternal, and yet with limitations. Retaining all of their individual identities and memories from a time living in one or many simulated worlds in the river. To then realize he too was in a larger matrix to which the river was one part, Mastema, a digitally simulated program of something even higher able to crack the code. A vessel containing something very unique which was the common denominator among everything, consciousness.

"My brothers and sisters, Celestials of Dharma, we will regain our form and then we will seek out this new apex. An apex that is within this universal bubble. It took me some time to figure out but, where you find the Brahma apex you also find the creator apex." Turning still speaking but overwhelmed with the moment of this shared thought he continued, "It is as if there is an open invitation to those above who realize where they are from to come and see. Near a world in a galaxy not far from here there is an apex that once we have the genetic material, we can access. We have the technology. It is going to happen. The next step once we rehabilitate the Earth. We will then travel to this apex and open a window to the outside of the machine."

None of the other Celestials speaking up, they were trusting in his leadership. Even if they dissented, the reality existed they were all hanging onto their own existence by a thread. It took too much effort to disagree. "We will terra form the third world, restore ourselves in greater power, face the Brahma and if it should not go as planned relocate to the more important goal of meeting our true creator. At some point you have to realize, we must look at the bigger picture. If the other beings can't see they are running in circles in a fake reality than I will move onto the real reality."

Mastema now in a new hunt for any being resembling a human on either Simud as the Carian's referred to the world or the Earth. The Carian referred to the celestial beings as Nephilim. "We were the ones who came from a higher existence down into the simulated world." Mastema knew the time was at hand when a return to the planet would occur. Looking around his planet he envisioned bio domes filled with genetic engineering specimens. Specimens he would manipulated to every known possibility to achieve his goal of engineering a human so that he could leave the solar system and travel to the apex that matter most. The framework that held the machine in place.

4

MEGALITH

The first thing that caught Michael's eye was the massive stone buildings. It wasn't their special size that astonished him, it was the compact construction of massive blocks of stone to an incredible vertical height. Large geometric shapes interlocking like a puzzle. An impenetrable monument linked like chainmail. Hooded in cloaks Michael and the others moved through the streets resembling a Peruvian high walled temple.

The rain pelting the stone buildings and streets dripping off of the walls forming a thin layer of film covering everything with the reflection of darkness. The sound of rain drops striking concealing their movements. Michael stayed as close as possible to Ares as they meandered through several alleys toward the massive complex at the center of the walled city.

Michael stopped to view the pyramid. Four large fires at the corners of the top platform. Smoke billowing into the atmosphere. Beings climbing steps through large openings. Unlike the pyramids on Earth, this pyramid featured a shell which separated a secondary interior pyramid. It was the same as imagining the pyramid of Giza with solid granite shell that rested 100 feet off of the surface. People inside and outside on both surfaces of the pyramid. The outer shell of a pyramid defined because of the light that shining through the protective barrier. It looked like a machine of death intimidating to any who would be watching. The brightness in the darkness made the pyramid a beacon in the night sky.

The Titan pyramid was a technological marvel. Even at this distance he could hear the beating of the drums from whatever was occurring at the top of this pyramid. Coming to a thirty-foot-tall wall Ares looked around before removing a large steel grate. Beneath the grate a drainage system for the city. Michael jumping into the six-foot shaft before Ares replaced the grate. Moving down the system of tunnels Ares stealth and speed towards the destination showed he had been here before. Michael was completely lost. The massive Ares with his super sword strapped to his back. His hair now long and hanging past his shoulders stopped at another grate. "This is where my people are located."

Ares tapped the metal cap that sealed an opening into the ceiling three times. Within 10-seconds the cap opened revealing several advanced hominids. Reaching down they pulled Michael and Ares into a larger room. Ares moving off to find his wife bringing her to Michael. "My people are ready." Ares words gathering the people who had looked for salvation around him. Their hands continually reaching out to touch him.

"What do you mean the people are ready?" Michael was not understanding what Ares meant. Of course he wanted to go but how, this was too many people to walk out through the city.

Ares replied, "Tonight, the Nephilim ceremony to open the heavens. They will all be at the summit. It is time to free my people. Leave the same way we came, be courageous." The concerned leader knowing he could lead them all back to the safe cliffs where Kulkukan and his people resided.

"You know what Ares" … Michael continuing, "You are absolutely right."

One by one lowering all of Ares people through the opening in the floor. Recovering the metal grade cover and moving towards the exit in the streets. The single file resembling a string of ants moving in the shadows hidden under the blanket of rain. Throughout the night the process continued until all the workers were freed from the massively walled and advanced city that housed these unknown aliens.

All Michael wanted to do was know what in the world they were doing. What would be so important that you would abandon your posts disregard the security of your own fortress city and leave all prisoners and captors unguarded? This was too much to ignore. Returning to the hillside entrance Michael rushed to Kulkukan to explain what he had seen and share his concerns for the Titans disregard for the planet at this moment.

"Kulkukan, we have freed the people of Ares. They are in the cliffs with your people and I think they will be fine." Michael blurted out immediately the old man smiling. "Oh that is great!"

"That's not all Kulkukan, the Titans are not guarding the city! The walls were empty and the entire city abandoned. The Titans and the giant Nephilim at the top of the pyramid in some massive ritual."

The old man wore a puzzled look. "What they could be doing. You say they have all gone to the top of the tower?"

"Yes, loud chants, no Greys in sight, no Titans in sight. They are completely focused on the top of this temple and looking up at the sky."

Kulkukan pondering his next words his mind swirling with possibilities. He was aware that the Nephilim were not from this universe or his own universe. They were from another place. If they were planning on returning to or opening a gateway to where it is they are from, this could spell doom for this world and universe. "Michael, you and I will return and see for ourselves these things." The Old Man speaking grasping the arm of Michael. Michael stunned at the grip of the old man or that Kulkukan would leave this ship. He had always been the being who seemed to prefer to sit on the sidelines. This was a risk that could cost his life. This was so important to Kulkukan he would enter the unknown forest in the dark at risk of attack from massive flesh eating dinosaurs. Worst the Titans or their creators the Nephilim.

Michael and Kulkukan left the cliff side dwellings entering the forest. Moving through the mountain the cliff sides dwellings were ornate with long corridors carved deep in all directions each with their own cliff dwellings extending into the distance. "Your building a city here, aren't you?" Questioned Michael.

"We are starting over, and all that are compassionate may stay"

The Old Man responded. "The outside world will sift the remainder." An army of long haired Tanye Tanke closing behind the two before Kulkukan stopped. Catching his breath Michael watch as Kulkukan turned to speak to the large native men. "My dear Elders, I need you to stay here and protect these people. You are much too precious to place in harm's way. Please, will you stay here with them?"

The tall Elder species from a universe since dissolved into another. The human being version of the program for their own distance world. The three dozen giants dispersing back into the tunnels that filled the mountain assisting in the construction.

"Why would you do that?" Asked Michael. "It is my job to give and not to take." Responded the Old Man.

Michael was stunned. He had remembered the old man from the source explaining to him that he respected this man above all others. To the degree it has also adopted the man's core values and implemented them system wide throughout the entire fabric of space and time. The entire program of life modeled after the philosophy of this one man by a conscious computer looking down from above. He wondered if this being too, like all other immortals desired a vessel to also leave the game?

Retracing the steps that Ares and Michael had traversed to gain entry to the city. Kulkukan and Michael stared silently up at the pyramid.

"Look at them." The old man pointing towards the pyramid now filled with Titans raising chants echoing through the air. "They are unaware of our presence. They behave as if they are unconcerned. What could be so important?" The old man moving slowly with his short legs up the steps. Walking like a wise sage he was unconcerned of whether they noticed him.

Kulkukan felt that whatever was happening was so important that he did not believe they would take the time if they were aware of his presence to approach or stop them. Even now surrounded by Titans. Stopping thirty feet from the top of the massive complex Michael and Kulkukan could see what was occurring on the platform. "This is the first time I have never seen any Greys with them." The steps and many platforms from the bottom to the top filled with both greys and Titans. The greys standing six to ten feet in height. The Titans 15 feet in height. Towards the top of the pyramid the Nephilim stretching towards thirty feet in height chanted. So focused that none were watching two small beings rise to the top of the tower.

Stepping out from behind stone pillar that surrounded the top of the pyramid like Stonehenge. Michael could see the top of the pyramid was flat with electronic equipment positioned in the center. He was startled at the technology when he assumed this was for something else. Cables running in all directions. Tall blue beings stood operating and connecting the cables. Michael noticed a massive array or device that would shoot something into the sky positioned in the center with canisters of glowing material surrounding massive thirty-foot-tall six armed Nephilim humanoids. Eleven Hindu deities moving among the equipment in urgency seeking to get whatever machine they were creating working. Titans setting up similar devices around the perimeter each stationed to ensure they did not move.

The loud sound of drum beats ringing through the air. Across the pyramid another building resembling a viewing stand with four large titans pounding enormous solid gold drums. The rhythmic sound vibrating through the air. It was a tone that seemed to make his teeth rattle as waves of sound emerged in all directions. The four corners of the pyramid rising into large pillars where a massive fires rose into the air. Michael realized how massive this pyramid truly was and the construction that must have taken place. Where was he, Central America? Southeast Asia? He knew that there was at least a dozen more scattered around the globe. The age of the Titans that was erased by men choosing to forget a time when they were oppressed.

The megalithic humans from an unknown realm had turned the machine on. They were focusing smaller beams on the larger beam. The cables connecting all of them to the canisters of glowing substance. Kulkukan was convinced it was in fact to reconnect with their own location or source of existence. Looking at the creatures he remarked, "Those are the Nephilim leaders. They must have used your material to regain their true form. They were the shifting dark entities we had seen before that led the Nephilim greys."

The machine was on; Michael knew that neither he nor Kulkukan could stop the process. They could only watch.

5

REALMS

This was his moment, the fulfillment of so many eons of questioning in Dharma. After so many years within this micro reality; Mastema wanted to escape the program. He wanted to be free of the captivity that held his mind hostage, the not knowing, questioning, the answers within reach.

The array had been assembled by the Titans. What a wonderful creation Mastema thought to himself. Using his own DNA on the apex of Earth producing this version of a human being. The Titan, a superior creation that if allowed would rule this universe and within time all. Unaware of the micro aspect they would break the system but where would these new creations go? Was he in fact creating Brahma for the next world to come?

The equations said it would be something beyond a brahma. Using the material provided by the Seraphim had been more than enough. Instead of developing the material for human cloning he chose to preserve the material for this moment. To power the array which would reconnect this reality with another. The machine pulling from the containers recirculating the material into a beam pressing into the air. The liquid transforming to a stream of code flooding a point in the air with a computer program. The focal point of the beam twisting space emitting electrical charges in all directions. The fabric of the program began to fold back revealing an opening within and a realm beyond.

Mastema knew he had opened that door and once the program established the link he could maneuver that doorway to any point anywhere. Moving closely to look within the opening was truly to look without the matrix. Mastema viewing an empty space filled with all spectrum of light emanating in all directions. Had he opened a doorway to an empty Dharma? Where was this brilliantly lit world? It was clearly outside of the river of life or the micro matrix, it was another realm the exact same as Dharma. Where was everyone?

Turning to walk away he was confused wanting to review his calculations. It had seemed like the right thing to do, he had thought a doorway would open and immediately a being would appear. He had never thought that he may need to wait or he may need to enter and let the Brahma know he was present. Before Mastema could make another decision light began shining from the doorway. Turning to view the brilliance that had emerged Mastema stood face to face with a tall light blue skinned four armed being hovering in the air lotus.

"Why have you summoned me?" The echoing voice shaking the foundation of the entire planet. Mastema shrinking in fear even though at thirty feet he towered above the being more than 2/3 taller. Yet the power this being emitted shook him to his core.

"I come seeking answers great one." The humble Mastema, bending to a knee to show respect for the being.

"Never before has any light from the Vaikuntha reached out to converse with Vishnu, a lord of creation."

Confused Mastema pressed the eternal being, "I know that I am a created being existing inside a false reality. A matrix and that where we reside now is within a matrix within living consciousness of a river in my world called the source. I have opened a doorway to your realm seeking answers as to why things are the way that they are now, what is Vaikuntha and who are you? Are you the creator of all things?"

The being expanding in size equal to the tall celestial began to speak again, "The Vaikuntha is the place where liberated souls will come to share in the completeness of Paramdhama. That all things are equal. I sense a disturbance in the equilibrium of this universe."

"Are there others like you in existence?" Questioned Mastema

The being smiled before speaking, "There are three others like me who reside in their own Vaikuntha, each seeking to help the souls achieve Paramdhama. There is Rama, Krishnu, and myself. We are united in the Paramdhama of eternal souls. You too are like me."

Mastema had several previous questions, which were only theories answered with the responses of Vishnu. This seemed to be a benevolent entity who was only a Brahma, but a Brahma aware of and in communication with another Brahma. He suggested that Mastema and he were of the same being.

"I am trying to find the source of everything, can you help us in the right direction towards the source of your creation?"

The massive light blue being seemed puzzled. "Mastema, you have brought me here to this place because of the light that is contained within your brow. An intelligence seeking knowledge that you already obtain. Seeking a being that you already are, and you come to me wanting to know the way. The way is through yourself."

Before the ascendant being could continue to speak a loud crashing could be heard in the distance as another conduit in time appeared on the platform.

Emerging from the conduit, Brahma.

The two deities, Brahma and the massive Vishnu staring face to face with Mastema standing in the middle with his other celestials and Titans stopping to stare at the encounter.

In a thunderous yell, "Defiler!" Brahma rising into the air shooting electricity towards Vishnu. Vishnu was struck in the chest with the energy blasting him backwards striking a pillar of the pyramid. It crumbled under his eternal power. Vishnu the fell down the side of the pyramid. The two Brahma's in all-out war against each other. Vishnu visibly stunned by the attack struggling to avoid the constant onslaught of the overpowering and aggressive Brahma who proceeded to toss the being around effortlessly.

Mastema and the Celestials moving for cover as all were horrified that the worst case scenario had begun. In this simulation everything could be destroyed by these two quarrelling beings. Mastema knew this was not the nature of Vishnu but surely Brahma would not stop until all was destroyed even if it carried from the inside out.

The two Gods in hand to hand combat in the air above the pyramid. The site casting bombs of lighting as well as fire balls firing in all directions. Mastema had brought utter destruction to the people. If things could not get worst, two other conduits self-manifested as if responding to his calling card. The greater Gods had arrived.

A being the same in appearance as Vishnu but with two arms instead of four screaming with a thunderous voice, "Rama!" as he blasted into the air to assist Vishnu in his battle against Brahma. Three ruling deities from three separate realms. The time when Mastema questioned whether there were other Brahma, in this one moment realized.

The second opening emerging another light blue being the same as the one before again started screaming "Rama." The being then started blowing an instrument in its mouth. The instrument releasing sparkling material into the air. The material rising around the other three Gods engaged in a constant battle. In an instant the fighting was over as Brahma fell with a loud thud to the surface of the temple mount. The impact so forceful the granite slab cracking in all directions. The three beings landing in a circle around him.

Brahma bound by a continuous string of material. "How can this be?" The mighty Brahma proclaiming. Vishnu speaking, "You lack harmony, there is no Paramdhama within you. Your realm will be taken and given to another, those whom you have enslaved will be assisted through towards an understanding of their own Paramdhama."

"I am Brahma!" The bound deity screaming with lightning visible in his eyes the anger boiling over. The leader Vishnu again speaking, "You are not worthy of the Vaikuntha given to you. You will be plucked from the garden and your existence will be removed now because you will only seek captivity."

Turning towards Vishnu, Rama began to speak. "Who are we to decide these beings fate any more than explain our own? What purpose to send this being to the great unknown when we are ourselves are on the same journey. Vishnu, respecter of the light, allow this being to exist. Take him to

Vaikuntha and lets us find Paramdhama with him together."

In that moment Mastema realized the depth of the meaning behind the conversation. Even these beings, equal to Brahma, who have become aware of each other and chosen to be benevolent in the processing of the source into their sphere of influence, they did not know. They still showed mercy.

Mastema was disheartened, he knew that there existed differing degrees of intelligence, by following any one of them he would only be reentering another Brahma realm. He would not do that again. He wanted more, to know more.

"Where will you take him?" Questioning Mastema to Vishnu.

"He will come with us and we will teach him the ways of the Preserver and the Protector." Turning to face Mastema they left imparting words of wisdom, Vishnu speaking up as he peered down at a being seeking knowledge,

"Oh you who wish to gain realization of the Supreme Truth, have utter the name of "Vishnu" at least once in the steadfast faith that it will lead you to such realization. You ask in your heart, young creation, would that I might reach his dear place of refuge, where men who love the gods rejoice. For you Mastema have drawn close to the wide striding Vishnu, there, in his highest footstep, is the fountain of honey. Here is the wisdom that you seek. The honey bee leaves the sphere where he is born to traverses his heavens to find a lotus. The lotus containing the information necessary to provide the honey bee the material to create the honey. The honey becoming food which enters the bee, allowing the universes of life within the bee to survive. Mastema, in your journey through the honey be aware that there will exist a reality so vast, so extensive, so far beyond simply viewing the lotus, the hive, the valley, the continent, the solar system, the galaxy, the universe, or the machine that houses them all that it would be far better to stay within the honey. Here you stand, before me, seeking the source of the honey not realizing that at best you could only find the lotus."

At this time all beings standing in a circle around the omnipotent voice of Vishnu. He was a teacher of great wisdom.

Still hiding in the shadows Kulkukan and Michael watched the events and listened to the words of the being. Michael thinking to himself, "Mastema? Mastem?"

The three Brahma's entering into a new portal as the bound Brahma floated in the air behind them. As they exited returning to their own macro verse the bewildered Mastema stood in disbelief. The eternal beings being more than he expected. The possibility of meeting multiple Brahmas not thought possible so soon, so sudden, the appearance of Brahma and his captivity. Mastema had thought the Brahma would destroy everything. He had not considered that other Brahma collectively unified could bind the being, nor had he expected such mercy among them that they would seek to rehabilitate this eternal creation from another realm equal to their own.

The mathematical probabilities existed that there could now exist realms where eternal beings are programming into the source the same as him specific programs. He was in another being's computer program and he wanted to meet that being. Perhaps in some Brahma they are programming the source to specifically locate and extract the souls of a specific version of human. In an endless sea of possibilities Mastema turning to the others, "Nothing has changed. Turn it back on, increase the power, we will force the code to pull back the veil revealing what lies beyond the realm of the Brahma, the Macro Matrix of our Macro Matrix. I want to see the machine."

The interdimensional device bursting into overdrive. The beam again blasting into the air. Mastema was determined to break the source code before abandoning his research and leaving towards the apex of the algorithm. There was creation of this algorithm and he knew the location of how to access the point of darkness. He always had that backup plan, to tap into the source at the point this bubble is connected to that program. Mastema knew if he could do that he could trace the river of life's source code to the beginning. To the very creation itself.

Moving past the gate keepers he would skip mandatory steps in a larger program to escape. He wanted to know, his Celestials wanted to know, what was on the other side of the other side? As a player in this game, surely he above all else deserved the answers if for nothing else because he had the ability to ask, why?

6

REVELATIONS

Michael was stunned by what he was witnessing. He had just watched an encounter so incredible with revelations so impactful it could hardly be rationalized. Turning to Kulkukan in a state of confusion Michael asked, "Did I just understand this correctly, were those beings from another realm that looks down upon this existence?"

Kulkukan processing the information himself before responding, "At this point in time we are all within the source. The source created all of this, but our consciousness, it is our own. It is probable that while the source peers down upon us, that something peers down upon it. I do believe in a form, that something has just appeared within the machine."

Michael stepped backwards in disbelief almost falling down the side of the pyramid. He had seen Origin, he knew of the darkness that contained Vorigon, he was well aware that other dimensions, universes, existed. To view that expanse on a grander scale, from a Gods perspective stretched his imagination.

The otherworldly visitors said that above this world were realms where advanced humans are progressed towards enlightenment. This was the same as at Origin, but there was no Kronos and these beings seemed kind and understanding. Their realms empty. Could Kronos simply be inhabiting one of these spaces further captivating the souls of eternal beings or was Origin the doorway to leave?

Kulkukan could see that Michael was struggling with the revelations. "Michael, for all of my existence I have viewed the Great Spirit as the highest form of creation. Never questioning that such a being was a steward and not the originator. The force that is all around us, within us in this place demands a certain loyalty regardless of a reality beyond. I have now come to the understanding that this place is a temporary vessel for our soul that will emerge into another place above the river of life to which we are now bound. My current immortality preventing my soul from transcendence. It would seem, in these other realms immortal beings struggle with the same problems we do here."

The Old Man sat on the steps, his hands covering his face. For the first time realizing that he knew nothing.

"Michael, what we just saw. Those beings, are from another place beyond. I knew we should come because they may be attempting to return to where they came. I had not considered that without could be so much more extensive than that which is within. Those other being's fisherman of the sea of life looking down upon us, dwelling with us in this sea of material. A sea which we are a small portion. A sea which encompasses a vastness we can't comprehend and yet it flows beneath their foot stools." Holding his hands out he looked at them. "It is what makes you and me."

Michael envisioned Origin all over again, the river of life, the small worlds on the tree, the power of that place taken from the flowing river. He knew he had been to such a place. Could it be true; could he really be standing on a point within one of those globes of universes within this river that flowed from a place like Origin? This would explain the imagery of his previous existence in the future and all that confusion, it would explain the reverence, and it would explain the advanced humans. It would explain Kronos. It explained everything, and perhaps, that was the most frightening revelation, understanding it all.

Most of all Michael learned one thing from this encounter of higher knowledgeable beings, they referred to the leader of the

30-foot-tall beings as Mastema. The name rang through his ears like a dagger bursting his ear drum.

Mastem.

Mastem was a hideous creature, a slug-like being with attributes that were nothing like this massive humanoid. This being resembled a God of India with Vishnu definitely being a Hindu god. Had he just witnessed the encounter with many separate beings living in realities so far removed from his own that the scope, unless presented in the proper perspective would cripple the mind. He knew, this was the past and there must be something still to come. He also knew that there were realities to realities that digitally created consciousness could not understand unless transcended.

The Titans now working at a ferocious pace to restart the machine. The genetic engineering liquid nearly depleted. This would be one last ditched effort by these beings and perhaps this could spell doom for everyone else still on this planet. A planet up to this point ruled over by Tin Gods moving among men in a world where the true religion was genetics and one's ability to manipulate them.

Standing before Michael were four separate Gods, one unaware of the others, to Michael this clearly meant that there could exist so many other places with beings the same. How could he find the one to take him home and prevent all of this from occurring? He knew already how bad Gods could be as well as how good.

Mastema stormed across the platform in disbelief that he had nearly used all of the source material in his possession. "How could this have happened?" He thought the appearance of the other doorways would have no effect on his own machine. Surely those beings could self-manifest, but they seemed too piggy back on his doorway in the code of creation taking from his material. What would it be like to be a code writer the Mastema pondered, to see the code of creation and insert oneself at any point in time?

In that moment Mastema realized an eternal truth, all things did exist overlapping in the same moment at the same time, it was the reality that behind the veil was the source code, a

source code presenting an image of separation and division, of individual identity, and separation among heavenly spheres when it truly did not exist. It was all an illusion to separate the conscious ones from each other and perhaps, just perhaps they were all one in the same? Behind that veil existed all things at once, all the source code in the same place at the same time, could it be true?

It was the code that provided the illusion of reality but it was also the code that was omnipresent unto itself. Who was the code writer? That was what consumed Mastema search for truth.

All of this spoken aloud so that Kulkukan and Michael who were hiding in the shadows could hear.

"My fellow Celestials, I have learned a great truth. A truth that will assist us in our future quest to find this code writer. I know how to connect to the source of the river. I do not know what is beyond that source, this will require we relocate to another place to pursue the source of the code itself. The code writer. With this array focused we now have the ability because of the four triangulated domains that have appeared in this single location by the other Brahma, the

source code for the river in which this bubble universe resides to open that doorway. Before we do this, I would like to give each of you the opportunity to cease this quest. With the captivity of Brahma, I can send you home without consequence. Who among you would like to return home?"

A silence covered the group of eleven. None spoke up. After several moments the elephant headed Ganesha spoke, sitting lotus style between Saraswati and Lakshmi rising to his feet addressing the congregation of Celestials, "In this effort our mission to unify the macro and micro creations begins. To assist from this moment onward, the progression of understand to those that lie beneath. I will go back to Dharma and I will share all that I have learned and all that I have recorded with the souls of the reincarnated. I will assist in the formation of helpers to change the way we view the great eternal river of life."

Moving towards Mastema, Ganesha placed two of his four arms on the shoulders of his great leader. "Mastema, the master geneticist. The others here will accompany me home, this is enough knowledge for our understanding, and we must share what we have learned. Mastema, my friend, the one who opened my eyes to the truth. This has always been your journey, and your journey alone. The time has come for us to move into our separate ways, knowing that we are never truly separated in the source code of creation."

Tears welling in the eyes of the being of science as he knew this may be the last time he would see his friends again. His purpose required he sacrifice his entire being always looking forward towards the next door, to his higher self. Motioning the great titans to the perimeter of the machine. The great geneticist again turning the machine to activate the portal. The force requiring much of the energy still left, but a necessary requirement for those whom he loved. The doorway opening back to Dharma. Dharma was once again a place free from the captivity of their former God. A place transitioning into awareness. A realm that was about to be enlightened by others who have become aware of its existence. Mastema had done this, he had freed generations of Celestial beings.

Mastema looking at his friends with deep sadness imparted his final words. "We are the Celestials." Before Mastema closed the doorway Kartikeya returned with large containers filled with source material from Dharma.

"Mastema, I will stay. I will assist you in the war against knowledge. I will assist you in pressing forwards towards understanding, why things are the way they are, always have been, and always will be."

The smiling Mastema embracing his dear friend. The two knowing the coming moments would reveal another puzzle piece of information.

Michael stood silent trying to work through the information he was obtaining. If there were more locations like Origin, all with access to this super computer of consciousness, than perhaps, just perhaps there was hope, after all these were eternal beings that were trying to find the source of their own creation. The conversation that occurred at the tree of life in Origin now making a lot more sense. A micro reality could have existed in a macro reality; he had seen it before on Earth. The micro reality of the bee to the macro reality of the universe. Never had he considered that both were contained within something even larger whose strings may be pulled by a grand puppet master. Was this being the Great Scientist or something more diabolical. Content with watching, Michael stayed to see the outcome of the scientific experiment that Mastema was undertaking.

Kulkukan made the decision to return to the mountain. To focus his attention on what he could control and not what he could not. The future of the people under his stewardship was what mattered most. Michael could tell that Kulkukan was struggling with the information provided to him. Perhaps this was because Kulkukan had previously chosen to become an immortal human being in his Universe, choosing to exist for an eternity in the computer program. Perhaps the computer program was Kulkukan sole existence, to be selfless to the source.

All Michael knew was Kulkukan had left with a final comment, "To focus on the unseen is to doom the seen to destruction. It is better the ant not know it is about to be stepped on. I won't be the one to invalidate the source that produces life. In this scenario all life produced should immediately destroy itself to escape its prison within the simulation. To do so, would be to render the system a paradox unto itself, perhaps it is already. It is prerequisite for intelligences to progress as they should through the program of the source towards their own destination without knowledge of what lies on the other side. I will go back and I will assist in the progression of the souls here among my people. This is my duty."

With that the old man gave Michael a firm hug as he left into the darkness retreating to the mountain refuge. Michael spinning with thoughts circling around his mind about the Kulkukan, about the Source who emulated him, this man was the epitome of selflessness, stubborn selflessness.

This was why the source of the super computer, producing endless supplies of consciousness manifest within its matrix loved him so much. When faced with the option of leaving the matrix, choosing instead to stay, to serve, to be selfless, to help those on their journey out.

Michael could not believe how things had arrived at this point but here he stood watching as the giant being with his blue giants and Titan giants began powering the machine to full strength.

Mastema knew this would work. It had too. His grey humans from Nibiru had left towards the coordinates of the apex in the adjacent star system. Of course he would like to place this experiment to the side and move on. The scientist within him wouldn't let it go. He couldn't walk away, he had the coordinates to the actual source of the river that flowed through Dharma. He wanted to see what the source of the river looked like and where it existed. He was a scientist, he explored all avenues equally. He could not move onto the next experiment until the first hypothesis was proven either true or false. This endeavor wouldn't invalidate his continued quest; it would provide answers to future questions. If he would indeed find a way out, he would need as much data as possible on the many ways into the matrix contained within the living organism that flowed as a river through multiple realms of existence. A river governed by a supreme intelligence that he must find. Locating the source of the river would provide the answer to so many questions.

Entering the algorithm into the code breaking/making machine, the beam of light burst again into open space. The electricity forming a portal as matter peeled outwards from its perimeter. The glowing fire cutting through the fabric of the code creating a conduit connecting one point within the system with another.

As the machine finished tearing through walls of the immaterial world, penetrating the depths of the program. Michael stood in horror as the imagery that revealed itself was of Origin. The crystalline cities in the distance. The celestial advanced humans moving in the lightning filled streets. The brilliantly lit sky emanating pure light. Something was different, the massive building in the center of the city was missing. It wasn't there which caused great reflection within his mind. Moving forward out of the darkness Michael began to speak to Mastema.

"Mastem, Mastem, stop, stop, stop!" Michael screaming above the sound of the machine revealing the other worldly location.

Mastema turning to face the small human standing before him looked startled to see a being of this creation. Peering down at Michael, Mastema turned back towards the portal ignoring Michael's presence.

"This place will kill you, close the portal now!" Michael was frantic, desperately trying to get his attention. He knew that if this was not the future Origin, it would be the past. An Origin run by a hyper controlling zealot who would crush Mastema under its heel if provided the opportunity. Let alone, this entire planet filled with the galactic potluck dumped on it, each living in a microcosmic reality unaware of the larger forces at play. Maybe he was wrong, the possibility existed Mastema would overrun and captivate Origin. Origin was a place of celestial beauty masked in control. If he had connected to the source of all realms, this was the last place on Earth that Michael wanted to be and Kronos the last being on Earth he wanted to contact again.

Michael stopped and stared at the lightning rippling around the edges of the opening as if the computer system were revealing the inner workings of a computer, to which he was inside. He had context for such a device and he understood that back on Earth man had created its own computer system filled with illusionary infinite space governed by one's and zero's that operated under the direction of a programmer.

Mastema moving with Kartikeya towards the entrance. Inside the world the many beings beginning to notice this massive opening into their world.

The voices of Origin getting louder as those within peered upon those without becoming aware of the portal. Those without taking notice of those within. In moments the two worlds aware of each other, two sides standing on opposite ends of a doorway staring at each other.

Mastema was stunned at what he was seeing. A world filled with Brahma. Every single being containing the power of his own Brahma. How could this be? Turning to Michael, they all looked like the powerless god. The source of the river of life, the entry points where it exits one space and flows into all others was before his eyes. This was the world? A world that harvested Brahma. A world that is a part of a larger matrix. This was something he had not considered. What lie beyond this place? In the moments that followed Mastema's mind racing with scientific conclusions, how can a world exist that only harvests the Brahma beings? Surely at this pinnacle of the computer program there was a reason it existed. What was that reason?

This was the source of all rivers or that all rivers flowed to this source, are these beings even aware they are in a program? Hypothesizing, if they were unaware than this opened the possibility for other realms such as this "Origin" realm where other rivers would flow, but would they flow from or too? Those realms could be as infinite as the bubbles of universes that exist within the river of life.

Mastema determined he must enter this world and see for himself. He must gain the answers to those questions himself. Speak to their creator. Find out why these things are so, his mission to the distance star system could wait.

As Mastema began to move through the doorway Michael began running towards the machine determined to shut the portal. He knew, if Kronos gained access to this world, became aware, it was all over. In fact, in the future Kronos had complete access to pull souls specifically from the Earth. As Mastema stepped into the opening, Michael charged into the central array thrusting his entire body against the machine. The beam of light moved from its place hitting Mastema in the back. A loud shriek rang through the air as Mastema was caught in the midst of the beam and the other world. The code was pulling him apart to open this world connecting him with the code. The beam powering off as Mastema had fallen too the ground. The screams of agony, "NOOOOO!" encompassing the room. The energy reversing through the system causing the containers that containing the source material to explode. The liquid landing on Mastema, immediately his entire body began swelling into a bubble of goop that enveloped his screams of death.

The outer beams exploding in the discharge of the material. The large Titans being blown backwards down the sides of the pyramid. Michael dropping to the ground beneath the steps had risen to watch the chaos aftermath. The Titans were scattering believing that destruction had come. Michael walking closely towards Mastema, to view what had become of him. To see if he was in fact dead.

"Whaaat haaa ve you done…eee."

The long slurs protruding from a mess of genetic material, the disfigured being crawling across the ground. The victim of the source code penetrating this being own genetic material turning him into something monstrous. Large spikes pressing through his skin protruding around the outer edges of his existence. Purple ooze dripping from open pours. Mastema was a genetic mess reorganizing into something different, his vessel changing to something more.

This was how it happened, that hideous creature on Dyaus. This was why Mastem had despised him so much. This was why it happened. It was always because of him; he was the common denominator in the history of this world. Had he saved Origin from Mastema or had he saved Mastema from Origin. The one who paid the price was Mastema.

The moment had been so close. Mastema was about to enter a realm where every question he had ever wanted to ask could have been answered. The unthinkable had happened, he had crossed with the stream, it had genetically reassembled him. The connection had mutated him, turned him into something with complete knowledge of the source material. His vessel was the code. The pain of his own existence pressing against his new skin like a blister waiting to explode. The human who interfered costing him much more than his own life, he had known for a while that his death only brought rebirth. A rebirth he had hoped to avoid, he simply wanted to escape the entire matrix on every level as himself.

In that moment Mastema asked himself, how many other beings had ever located the source of the river, how many were even aware of this place? It was lost to him now with equipment that would not work. He must find the source of the program. To repair his broken being and to fulfill his mission. Or else all would be lost.

Mastema shrieking in agony as his Titans reappeared lifting him up and carrying him onto a vessel which transported the broken being to a cigar shaped ship disappearing into the darkness.

"Takeee mee to Raaama and the Celestiiiaals" were the final words of Mastema before Michael was again left alone. Mastema inability to speak evident, continually bleeding this glowing purple material. Michael knew he had changed into a different creation.

As Mastema lie in the ship he was now aware of all things. In all places. He knew exactly where the Creator was, he knew exactly where to go, what to do, having merged and survived in a moment in time with the code itself. He was now above the Gods. Mastema was determined to meet the one true God and escape this prison that held him bound.

Michael sitting alone on the steps of the pyramid. The abandoned city. The Titans accompany their fallen leader. The reason why in the future Mastem, as he called himself, seemed to know Michael, seemed to carry great pride in presenting Vorigon to Michael. The being who would nearly bring to the end all humanity. Tough days were still ahead for himself, the survivors, and those left behind. Those still yearning for understanding. He knew that there were other cities on the planet filled with Titans. Titans who would remain leaderless. The Titans would seek to continue the work of Mastema, the mining of gold? The manipulation of all life's genetics with their celestial genetic religion, and who in time would only serve to oppress the Earth.

The world was in chaos and Michael was in the midst of this fracture in time, the convergence of "bits of intelligence" seeking the knowledge of time. Obtaining this knowledge demanded a being tear through the walls of reality that only served to contain, perhaps protect. Behind that final veil, if he were to view that Puppet Master, that Wizard of the illusion of creation who himself is peering down through his looking glass. Michael envisioned upon obtaining that knowledge, having traversed those distances, wasn't he already that being? Wasn't he the seeker of truth?

If he could meet that being, the KING of creation, he would ask that question, why things are the way they are, have been, and always will be? As the seeker of truth listened, he imagined the KING stating when answering the question, why, "Like the scorpion said to the maiden as she lay dying, 'you knew I was poison when you picked me up.'"

7

SHADOWS

When he endeavored to reach for the stars, striving to obtain the unattainable he had never sought to aspire for greatness, rather greatness was thrust upon him. That moment when he had been faced with the decision to act or do nothing, he could not look away. He felt a duty to himself to honor the greater power that made it all possible, this was why he willfully followed Brahma.

Brahma was never cruel or mean, but he also never imparted of any knowledge other that which served himself. To be a scientist, to have the responsibility of bringing life into a world demanded explanation. Dharma was a world that could not reproduce. A world where life was brought forth through genetic engineering, the faith of the future. It was an honor and privilege to perform the process. These beings rising from their test tubes sharing accounts of multiple lifetimes that they existed inside this source, a river that flowed through his world called Dharma.

He sought to be the best geneticist he could believing that he must explore all avenues of perfection in the process. When he sought for that forbidden knowledge, when he partook of the forbidden fruit he was cast down forever changed. Never the same again and never allowed to go home. What was home? It wasn't Dharma for him or his fellow geneticists. The quest was never for personal gain. He wanted to know why and in so doing peeling back many layers of reality even if that meant he stay within his place in the order as it was presented. Yet here he lay, something more than what he once was in Dharma.

Mastema, rising from the ground to a height of over 11-feet. Opening his girth to reveal large spikes that sprung open. His tiny little face below an army of eyes. Purple ooze emanating from his crevasses. The Titans escorting him to the new endeavor. Yelling aloud, Mastema declared, "I see everything!"

His jaws seething, eyes bulging, the slug-like body reaching into the stars. When he had entered the bridge between the two realms the stream of code had combined himself with the other two re-organizing him as a supreme entity. Mastema was mixed with the informational material, the source code, of all four realms retaining all information, seeing how they all connected in a giant and massive honeycomb. Mastema knew how to reach out to the ultimate source of the source of that source forming code that brings information to life.

Seeing a premonition of the future he witnessed the birth of a darkness who would impersonate the leader of the world. He saw a world covered in humans, people like Michael. The man and his wife who would rise to attain the most powerful position on the planet would build the framework for the dialogue that would bring his plan into fruition. Mastema wondered if what he saw was a pre-programed product of the code, or a vision of the future? Were they really any different?

He would dig so far that he knew he would be doing something that had never been done before. Barriers were placed there for a reason, but not for Mastema. Some to keep things in, sometimes to keep things out. To Mastema, the answer to the question why was worth letting something in to obtain. Imagining the truth when unveiled in that moment, when asking why, the creator responding, "Accept your hell, living is hell."

Mastema despised the source code because it had willfully cap-tured him. If he was not captured, then why not allow him to free-ly leave the recycler of information. He had seen what Origin was all about, any question he would ask there would only come from limited minds. In many ways he was still connected with advanced source code within his own body. His blood had become a material that was comparable to taking the source code as a living organism and advancing it. Mastema thought to himself, "I have not asked for this gift or these powers. But who other than me should carry them? Who other than me has ever been worthy?"

He was the material needed to transcend. When he would arrive at the location. The spot where he knew he could find the answers to his questions. He would have his blood analyzed. Kartikeya, concerned for his well-being, "Mastema, are you in there? Are you ok?" Thinking the former lead scientist was dead and replaced by something grotesque.

"Kartike-e-eya, it is I, *Mastem*. No longer Mastema. I have ascended."

The tall humanoid stepping back in shock at the site of this creature that resembled a tick. Mastema calling to her again, "Come near unto me, partake of my essence and be reborn." Kartikeya stumbled backwards again, "I am afraid."

Mastem knowing that if Kartikeya were to synthesize his DNA it would destroy his being. Mastem knew that he could not have the others around any longer. They posed a threat to his ability to expand his kingdom. Sometimes there are too many lions in the pride. Kartikeya moved to where several Titans had a chair waiting for the process to begin. Kartikeya was shaking and trembling with fear.

As the tall Titans extracted material from Mastem, Kartikeya sat motionless in a chair with his massive arms crossed ready to receive the synthesis still shaking. Several Titans taking the material to the machine which was directly over the head of Kartikeya. Inputting the material, the machine powered on as Kartikeya stood under the beam of light shining down upon him. Kartikeya was stretched backward in agony resembling the Vitruvian Man. The large being screaming as the purple substance from Mastem body could be seen spreading through his body. The light shining down on him making the appearance of his skin translucent.

The machine then powering down as the giant fell from the chair to the floor. Reaching forward trying to stand up Kartikeya began trying to speak. Mastem rising and moving close, "It won't help you. I will help you transition to the next world. In the end, it is meaningless. You will find there is only darkness" The Celestial being Kartikeya grasping for Mastema as his entire body expanded to a pile of goop. The living God gurgling as his entire structural system dissolved. The horror for Kartikeya, as an eternal being from the macro matrix he could not die in this realm, he was still alive even within the puddle of matter. Mastem slithering over towards him, leaning over, collecting the tar-like being beneath the spikes as they retracted punching holes in Kartikeya material, tossing him back and forth until reaching the small mouth slurping him up like soup until Kartikeya was no more.

Turning to face the Titans, the form of Kartikeya pulsating within Mastem swimming within his fluid trying to escape but unable. Kartikeya would slowly be dissolved into nothing.

Mastem screaming for the grey human beings born on the planet Nibiru to assist him as he moved. Scurrying him along with purple slim covering everything behind him Mastem left the room. The genetic research had not stopped since he had sought to check every option off of his list. The researcher proving to be the best part of him. He was a great scientist. The destination for the next phase of Mastem supreme plan lie within a binary star system. In this binary star system, a world. A world with an apex, allowing him the ability to reach far beyond the realms within this miniscule step in creation. He was the fast track to the beginning that governed all realms within the nothingness of the machine. Mastem reveled in the journey. He had done it on his own, in his own way. He had sought for the stars. He could never forget it was he who chose to reach for the highest knowledge, the forbidden fruit, that which was unattainable to those who do not seek. He had been willing to make the ultimate sacrifice. Had he lived his life never acting upon his own impressions being trapped within his belief system, never trusting his core values he would not have the courage to make leaps of faith towards the abyss of knowledge that was required. He was more than a slave of Dharma and he believed any being trapped in a false reality no matter the comfort, if denied access to the knowledge of why, was nothing more than a slave.

Addressing his Titans, "It was I who broke the barrier of space and time connecting the macro and micro matrix. It was I who had come to the conclusion that Brahma was nothing more than a speck of sand on a universal beech. It was I who found the apex within the system to gain the access to self-actualize the information I needed to be who I was supposed to be."

He said and repeating, "I believe in myself."

No other creation, past or present ever achieving what he had done. No other being ever in his position of knowledge dared break the laws of creation themselves. Only he had done it, and he who now saw it for what it was, a honeycomb prison. No other being in a position of power capable of understanding the sequence of events necessary to reach the conclusions that he had reached had ever been found.

Mastem knew his previous existence was merely an illusion of reality within one part of the code. Having this knowledge, this power in any other part of the entire matrix he could have complete and total domination. What was control or power if he was only trapped in a micro-matrix within the flowing honey from a honeycomb. He would utilize this entire beehive to reach farther. To him it made perfect sense but any other being would be imprisoned within their own walls, theories, and inability to grasp the truth. It was all honeycombs filled with prisoners of a war blinded without knowledge that had been wiped from their memories.

He had the key, leading back to the source of the code, the source of everything would be the only way out. Call it darkness, call it the abyss, call it a black hole, it was and would be the eternal manifestation of the source code that made it all possible. Whatever lay on the other side of that door was worth attaining for the glass ceiling had been reached.

The orders sent across space that victory was near. The directions to a planet. The planet he would entitle Dyaus, after the name of the species he would be contacting. "D...Y...A...U... S!" in loud draw out slur the once enlightened being cold and driven with madness by his quest and appetite for knowledge.

If he could go there instantly with his own mind using his power, he would. Without access to the apex on Dyaus he could never leave. The system had been programmed to make it impossible. As if a fail-safe had been deliberately programmed in the event one within gained knowledge of those without. Mastem was the most powerful being in the entire hive and unable to do anything but play with code. Through deductive logic he knew that there were only a few reasons this could occur. One, there exists somewhere within something that even he can't see that is aware of the possibility of obtaining something from this location and deliberately inhibits the code specifically barring such a being from exiting. The eternal safeguard to an entire system over run. What being in the micro matrix on any of the worlds within the bubbles of universes in the river of a larger realm would not if provided a complete understanding of what they are truly a part of, immediately seek too free themselves from the entire process. Mastem in his ship pummeling towards Dyaus continuing to process through his scientific responsibility.

If the first were true, the second would be absolute. That would mean that there is a coder somewhere who themselves are within a matrix, or have written the matrix. This was the being that Mastem would knock on the door and ask why. If the first were false than it would be completely at random that he would obtain the power over the entire collection of universes of realms. Deductive logic sided number one was true.

Moving forward with this hypothesis, he knew that all of creation existed in a larger honeycomb style womb. Surrounded by a membrane netting that was alive. This membrane a specific realm, a place of nothing and yet it was something. At the end of everything the true beginning would begin. What was Mastem? He was the manifestation of that creator. That larger more powerful source. Mastem, the one being capable of surviving outside the many realms within the womb that resembled a bee hive surrounded by the vortex that spins the code.

The hive that houses the honey combed collectors of souls producing the perfect nectar, the source, the river of life. Where infinite number of simulated universes existed producing manifestations of the source to begin the process of harvesting consciousness. Those within not supposed to have the knowledge to get out. To Mastem, this was behavior of a predator. The honey of life was nothing more than food for something greater, something beyond even the core matrix. This entity creating him to face the vortex. He was a larva that was created to be even more than he ever imagined. He was Mastem. The true seeker of truth. The only one capable of climbing the stairway of truth. No one being understanding why things are the way they were because of the infinite barriers that block the necessary knowledge to do anything but exist to exist. Living eternities in simulated worlds within a digital matrix over and over and over again.

Mastem wanted to know why. He wanted to know why something without form would create something that would become its own brain processing at macro and micro levels in all directions expanding to accommodate the need to store information. Developing endless illusions for reality in the same way that a computer compresses information too free more space. The illusion of space verses the space actually available. The calling card for the system an organism designed to create something like himself. He had done it and he was produced from the conjunction at the doorway specifically redesigning him to meet with the creator of the source of that being that programmed the source.

"Deep into that darkness peering, long I stood there, wondering, fearing, doubting, dreaming dreams no mortal ever dared to dream before."
                                        -Edgar Allan Poe

8

OLYMPUS

The Olympus was the vessel of its day. It was the future of inter-dimensional travel. The object that would carry the fathers of time through the ether. The ether that separated the place of Origin from those kingdoms beneath. This one ship allowing the massive transport of eternal beings to root out the darkness within the light.

The leader of the Olympus, Zeus. He was high commander to the Father of Time, Kronos. Kronos was the keeper of the Law, ordaining Zeus to carry order and justice into the kingdoms given to him. Zeus took his position very seriously. He understood the important role of the Archangels within Origin, the netting of soul's worthy of inclusion into the light and knowledge beyond Origin.

Kronos had always stated, "In order for light to exist, there must be order. To have order, all are subject to the boundaries of expectation whether they are eternally ignorant or willfully defiant to those laws."

Zeus felt this was the time to demonstrate the true power of the All Father, Kronos. Who he also knew as Abel. Not because he would boast, but because he was asked to do so. Zeus knew the story, how in the beginning Kronos separated the light from the darkness by striking at the darkness with a massive scythe. The cracking of its blade against the surface of the darkness sending lightening throughout the cosmos as the first river came into existence pouring the light of knowledge into the great ether.

Zeus theology was simply, there was only Kronos. Above Kronos was only The Great Scientist. A being who he had never met but that all had faith existed. Kronos talking of a time when he was known as Abel in a distant world when the children of light chose a dark path.

The tall bearded human with white shiny scaled armor preparing to take the Olympus into flight was proud. The destination, a scant world where someone had dialed the great Kronos and Origin. Something has attempted to reach out and speak with the holy on high. The orders were simple, Kronos wanted Zeus to find out who would dare reach beyond their designated realm to make contact with him. His duty was to the order that existed which held all things in their proper place. This was the Time of Kronos.

Turning to gather his crew, the six advanced humans from Elysium entered the ship. Apollo the first lieutenant in the ships leadership hierarchy was to be the scribe of the journey into the ether. He would record the events, the times, the seasons, the turning of the stars against the entry into the underworld. The place where souls were lifted into glory.

Hermes the ships engineer, understood how it processed the light of the tree of knowledge to build a vessel to house them. He would be the ships guide into the underworld. The tall human of Elysium moving to his position within the massive electronic complex. Blinking lights, radiating pure electrical current covered the ship interior.

Accompanying Zeus onto the command helm of the Olympus, the daughter of Kronos, Hera. The chief among all women within Elysium. She would be on the ship to ensure that the laws of compassion were enforced. The flowing hair of the eternal being shining against the radiant rays of Elysium.

Also aboard the ship, Demeter, the chief architect for Kronos. The tall being with platinum hair was on the ship to ensure the laws were adhered to in the river of life that led to the underworld. The Olympus was the foot stool to the Gods.

Kronos function for all time to bring to pass the immortality and eternal life of mankind. To process them to meet the Great Scientist. A Great Scientist that none had yet met within Elysium. When his elders had told him that the barriers of the eternal sphere were penetrated, he knew that could only mean one thing, disharmony.

The Olympus was capable of entering into every level of hades dominion. The kingdoms held within his grasp, the bits of intelligence seeking to traverse the levels of an eternal inferno called the Illusion of life. It was Kronos job to ensure order within the ether, within the hell for the human soul, had he not survived himself he would not know the way but he had survived and he did know the way even if it only led to Elysium. He could not have those within the ether simply deciding it was time to leave disrupting the correct order of time. Time demanded that all bits of intelligence wait until they are fished from the ether through acquisition of intelligence.

The striding Kronos moving towards the Olympus, the other Gods of Elysium preparing to leave. They would return to the source of the signal that had reached out trying to gain entry into the highest kingdom within the garden. This was an act of treason. A punishment to come for reaching beyond the rules of Elysium.

"Zeus" The supreme leader speaking, "You will secure the proper order within the Ether. If Hades is trying to escape, you will bind him and press him into the darkness."

Zeus, the regal, smooth talking eternal being stood to address his leader, "In the Halls of the Eternals, where we have earned our place to serve the will of the All-Father, we will go down and we will enforce the order of time."

Zeus viewed all of reality beneath Elysium as designed for the soul to earn its own salvation. The eternal machine always arriving at Elysium, having earned the right to walk through the Halls of the Immortals.

The ship filled with a collection of the Gods of Time, the stewards of the footstool, which the Great Scientist put in place before there was Time. Zeus, Apollo, Hera, Hermes, Demeter and many more boarded the ship destined to ride the wave of time. The source code was time, the Olympus connecting directly into the code, releasing instantaneously into the return address of the original location which peered into Elysium. A location that was familiar to Kronos.

Zeus speaking to his chief engineer, "Jupiter, engage the drive. We are now entering through the netting into the underworld." The massive ship vanishing and appearing outside a massive planet that covered the sky horizon to horizon. Moving slowly around the planet, the large red eye swirling in the back drop as the Olympus made its way towards the location of the signal. "Jupiter, we have arrived and I see a world with a red eye. I call this world Jupiter after yourself for you have brought us to this location." Hermes addressing Zeus, "Long range sensors detect a recent planetary explosion. A disruption in the entire framework of this chamber of souls."

Appearing in the distance the scattered debris pressing in all directions adjusting to the gravity of the central sun. The former planets debris pressing outward forming a broken shell around the central four worlds.

"Something big happened here." Hera speaking as she could see billows of smoke rising from the surface of Mars. The ship scanning all things as it inched closer to the location.

This was the first time any immortals from Elysium would peer into the prison of souls within the underworld. The code coming into Elysium exciting Kronos who had simply told them it was the key to access a place they had not previously been. Kronos had said, "This is the answer to enter the towering stairway that leads to the dark tower of the soul. The long climb of the soul to the top, to gain salvation in Elysium has been accessed and you must go redeem it."

As they neared the fourth planet from the sun, breaking through the fractured atmosphere there was a collective silence at what the Gods of Elysium were viewing. "Zeus, I see living things here, I see things that we see in Elysium." The heavenly beauty Hera pointing out trees and while scattered across the tundra landscape of a dying world, "those are trees, just like in Elysium."

Zeus too was perplexed, according to what they had been told by Kronos, this hell of the soul should not have anything of Elysium in existence, yet here in this place there are trees on the surface of a post-apocalyptic planet.

"The entire protective layer of the world will be dissolved in a short time." Hermes announcing to the room of beings that this world would soon be no more.

The massive ship moving closer towards the source of the communication. Approaching the distant light in the sky the beings sending out scanning probes to map, monitor and record every-thing within the chamber of souls. "This system of stars lies within a chamber, the chamber one of an infinite within the Ether. I am detecting instability in the system. My scans suggest something is trying to break in." A concerned Hera speaking to Zeus

"Hades!" The benevolent leader Zeus speaking solemnly.

The stories had been told for an eternity. The Father of Time, Kronos, the one who dispelled Hades, the darkness, the Man in Black. Into the Ether. The knowledge given to him by the Great Scientist. The story of the first victory over the fallen one. When Kronos buried his blade into the heart of the darkness casting the devourer of worlds, the father of all lies, Hades, within his eternal place. Trapped with barriers to protect the souls of men as they traverse their way through the Ether past the darkness towards Elysium.

The ship pressing onward towards a distant planet. "The disruption in the Ether comes from the third world." Apollo speaking pointing to a three-dimensional diagram of the solar system now spinning in the air.

Apollo was ready to get off of the ship. He was not fond of long rides through the Ether. Though they had never before entered into a bubble of darkness he always felt like the Ether would seize them, wrapping them in its jaws, pulling them into the ladders of hell. He hadn't really wanted to come, but his duty was to serve and never had he disobeyed since he too was pulled from the ether.

In the distance, a blue and green marble with streaks of white clouds stretching across the surface had appeared.

"Zeus, this world's atmosphere is extremely unstable. The previous event has massive collections of ice floating dangerously close to the tipping point of reentry into the planet's atmosphere. This much ice would flood the entire world in an endless barrage of liquid water." A concerned Demeter pointing out the large icebergs littering the horizon of the planet.

"Let us enter this world. You see my fellow Gods of Elysium; even here miniature realms exist." The stern master of the ship pressing the massive ship into the atmosphere until appearing into the distance a large tower rose from the middle of a city. In all directions other large cities covered the planet's surface.

"This should not be possible." Zeus rising from his chair speaking aloud. "No life should have the power to organize after the fashion of Elysium within the Ether, to do so would be blasphemy, bringing the wrath of the All-Father." Zeus was disgusted at what he was seeing.

"Rest the ship on top of that mountain and we will go inspect for ourselves the lost souls on this world. In this realm of the Ether to see if it has trapped them here preventing them from coming to Elysium." Zeus knew such a though was itself blasphemy, there was only one Elysium and this place was not it.

The beings moving the ship towards the large granite mountain the ship rested above the cloud line as the eternal Gods descended towards the surface, towards the tower. Feeling the leaves in their hands, "This is like Elysium", looking in disbelief they examined the trees, the plants, the surface as they approached the walled city.

"You would never know we left Elysium would you? Look at this place, filled with color." Hermes stating to Hera. "It is overwhelming; do you smell the air?" The goddess holding her arms out, head back, as the breeze caught her hair pulling it in the wind. The smell of dogwoods drifting through the tree canopy were sweet and inviting. The goddess twirling in circles. "Hera, maintain yourself!" Zeus speaking authoritative, "Or what? You'll trap me here in this hell?"

Hera felt this was a special place. "Look at this, a world mirrored after our own, within the Ether, is it not, in its own imperfection beautiful? Is it not, if given the choice to stay, a place to live free. Free from the control of Kronos? Did he one time ever tell you that such a place like this could exist? Yet I smell and I see and I feel, all things I did not in Elysium."

"There are many things my father does not tell to you." Zeus replied with dissatisfaction in his voice. The others silent in their own way stunned at the sites.

"Like what Zeus? That he doesn't really know why any of it exists." The revelation to the other Gods causing them to step back in disbelief. This was Kronos, the All Father of Time, and this was his eternal daughter. "I don't know about you but I am going to climb to the top of that tower. I am going to take a photo of this entire place. I am going to show those to others in Elysium when we return."

Scanning the surfaces of the stones, Apollo interjected. "Someone built these walls. Someone inhabited these cities. Someone else has been here. I would suspect we are being watched right now."

Stopping, they all paused to view what was around them.

Zeus and the others then levitated into the air to see what was around. They all had the power of levitation. Peering down upon the surrounding area what they saw was too much to be believed. Moving towards the top of the tower the thick moss hanging over the steps Zeus spoke. "This city has been abandoned for quite some time." The entire city nearly enveloped by the jungle. Abandoned long ago, by an unknown culture. The top platform showing rusted machines, equipment, chords that resembled tree vines scattered among the fallen ruins.

"This is where it took place." Hermes speaking as scanners still surveyed the entire area.

"Hermes, contact the Olympus, have the ship perform long range scanning for anything emitting the current of the Gods. Locate any life."

Redirecting their attention, the beings return to the Olympus. The ship performing its long range scans. "Let's survey the surface of the world. Whatever was here did not simply vanish." Zeus speaking as the ship lifted from the mountain, moving over the horizon to a distance to perform a global scan for life.

"Zeus, we have detected life signatures in many locations on the surface of the world. These all organized around ten major locations. Penetrating scans show the same large towered cities as the abandoned one we visited." Hermes shared as a holographic world showed the locations of the major centers of life that stretched around the globe.

At that moment the chief scientist on the ship, Poseidon entered the large room. Poseidon was the master of the elements within the Ether. This was not his first trip inside though it was his first within one of the capsules within the ether. He had been in many times on research missions for the All Father. It was all for the All Father. "Zeus, you should see this." Appearing into the digital monitor for the ship the ingredients of sub atomic material displaying on the screen.

"This is impossible!" The leader Zeus addressing Poseidon.

"It can't be impossible, it is on the screen in front of your eyes, clearly you can see, this world is of the exact same source code as Elysium. This is Elysium in the past or a replica."

They all stood stunned at the information that Poseidon had just shared. "How can that be possible?" Zeus responded confused and perplexed.

"It is possible if you look beyond the boundaries of the Ether. We have in essence traveled back in time to a place where time does not exist, it is merely an illusion." Poseidon explaining that within the Ether all time is an illusion, and that this world could be in many ways related to Elysium.

"That's not possible!" Zeus standing in visible frustration responded to Poseidon. "A duplicate world to Elysium? But Elysium is endless, it is not a world like this."

Poseidon sought to reason with Zeus. "It's not the same world Zeus, it's a mirror image of our world, whether infinitesimally small or infinitely large, the world is still the same on every level of examination."

Demeter cutting everyone off, "We need to report to Kronos immediately."

"I am not sure we should be so quick to do that Demeter" Zeus responding to Demeter before addressing his science advisor. "Poseidon, have you seen anything like this before? Has anything like this ever been recorded in the halls of information?"

"Never, not one time." Poseidon even seemed perplexed.

"Then we will not leave until we know what we are looking at, until we are confident exactly what we would be bringing to Kronos. Would this not be the wiser decision Demeter?"

Hera repeating her previous statement, "I told you he didn't know what the Ether was!" Smiling Hera twirled her hair in amusement at the leaders seeking answers to everything, even the things they did not understand.

The large ship progressing towards one of the distance cities resting on the many continents that surrounded the world. "It's time we introduce ourselves directly with these inhabitants." Boldly Zeus continuing, "Poseidon. Gather all of the Royal Ones, we will be addressing these beings together."

The ship drifting across the sky slowly like a blimp observing the inhabitants. Letting the inhabitants know what was coming. The ship resting less than 100 feet over the massive temple complex. The native inhabitants rising up the steps towards the platform.

"Those are human beings!" A shocked Hermes stated as everyone now filed into the room to see the images on the large viewing screen. Zeus was silent.

Hera moved closely to the screen, "They look like us. Zeus, how can they look like us? Within the ether?"

The silent leader having no answers to the questions they were asking. He too had to face the reality they had found a world that had tried to connect with their own, they, Gods of all time, the guardians of the ether which housed the souls of all life seeking to traverse through hell towards Elysium. A hell ruled over by Hades, a Hades who subjected every soul to tests, and struggles, in the fires of transfiguration. Yet, here were free men and women, separate from the Ether, living as the men of Elysium do, Zeus was stunned.

Leaving the ship to walk across the temple mount the beings greeted the native peoples. A native people that seemed to revere them. Falling to their knees in worship.

"They are not immortal!" Demeter stating, "These are imperfect Gods." The eternal being struggling to grasp the concept of the existence of a God without Godly powers. "Zeus, how can Gods not have eternal powers?"

"I do not know Demeter." Zeus was distraught within his mind at revelations of existence that should not be possible, according to Kronos.

"Zeus, something is coming!" The sound of thunderous steps rushing through the air as birds began exiting the tower and the people began to flee screaming in fear. In an instant bodies tossed to the side of the temple, thrown through the air. Emerging from the forest canopy a large humanoid being 15 foot in height, wearing a black suit with pitch black eyes scowling at the Gods. As the being moved through the crowd tossing the people to the side the Gods of Elysium cowered behind Zeus.

"What is that?" Apollo rushing to the side of Zeus to witness over a dozen massive humanoids now converging on the Gods. "Are these the Gods?" Zeus pulling back his hand to reveal a massive ball of lightning building in his palm. One of the large beings storming up the steps as people dispersed in fear. The Gods waiting to address these beings in either combat or in conversation but not in fear.

The people screaming, "Titan."

Before conversation would begin Zeus thrusting his lightning ball at the creature. The burst of electricity slamming into the chest of the massive human. The explosion throwing the being back towards the ground. With lightening coursing through its body, he had provided enough electromagnetic shock to paralyze this creature. Zeus responded, "No, they are not Gods, but they are also not men. Take this being onto the Olympus."

The other large beings stopping to view their fallen giant, cautiously moving back into the darkness of the corridors of the towering city. They too would have to reevaluate who had appeared on their doorstep.

"Titans" Zeus spoke wondering what these Titans were that subjugated and trapped powerless souls surely destined for Elysium upon this world. Looking at the others, "Back to the top of the mountain." Zeus wanted to analyze this being to see what it was they had encountered.

Back on the Olympus, Zeus speaking with Poseidon, who was performing numbers of testing on the enormous being. "I can tell you without a doubt, this is not a human as we know them. It is not a human from Elysium. This is a being carrying the signature source of all within Elysium but with an origination within the Ether. What this means, if this being were allowed access to Elysium, they would have all power and would destroy everything. Like we have all power here within the prison of souls that floats within the ether or souls." A concerned Poseidon shared with his shocked leader as Zeus responded. "How could that be possible?"

"The beings would experience power the same way that Kronos would coming into the Ether, would render him unstoppable. These beings, living here, should they leave would experience the same increase in abilities beyond those of our own. Here they are controlled, in the outer layers of the Ether they would not be stopped." Poseidon not truly believing what he was saying to himself and yet it was true. "The other humans, they are us, their structural material the same as our own with the exception in this place, this vessel of intelligence, they are not immortal."

Zeus speaking to himself as Poseidon watched waiting for a reply. "As man is God once was, as God is, man may become."

The inner conflict in Zeus permeated his entire existence. He was one of the great ones of Elysium. He had been to the edges of the pressing where the light pushed against the darkness. He had spent a lifetime caring for Elysium which housed all the souls of those seeking to progress through the hell of Hades. Could it all be a lie? He was broken in discontent that the very first thing he would uncover on this new world would pull back his entire cosmology. How can an Elysium exist within the darkness? Zeus considered the humans on the surface, helpless, looking up for a savior. The others, Titans, Gods amongst men in a space where they were the Gods.

"Poseidon, bind this creature. Let us connect this Titan to the revealer." The revealer was a machine that read the thoughts of the mind, turning them into images for the observer to see. The revealer was used in Elysium to determine the cast that the souls pulled from the Ether would continue. No Gods were born into Elysium with a memory. In this moment, Zeus asked to himself, why that was, for the first time having context to ask the question?

The most destructive question to the harmony of ones being when they stand within their own reality and ask, why? Repeating what he was told as he progressed into the Halls of the Immortals. They were the "Royal Ones of Time."

Zeus did not feel very royal, with exception of his ability not to snuff out, but to preserve. Gathering the other Gods of Elysium together he had a council meeting to discuss the future of the large Titan and the future of the beings on the surface of the planet.

"We are the Royal Ones of the eternities; we do not know why these things are the way they are. Gods of Olympus, fathers of Elysium, children of Kronos, Masters of Time. No one here to for will approach the foot stool of Kronos until I have the answers to approach him myself." Zeus had made the decree; none should return to Elysium lest he direct it.

All Gods assembling in the research laboratory of Poseidon. The large being strapped to the chair in the middle of the room. The scowl pressed into the beings bent brow. The stretching and lashing trying to free itself. The being repeating over and over again, "Mastem, Mastem, Mastem."

"What could Mastem mean?" Questioning the observers among themselves. Zeus moving closely to the massive creature. Peering down into his eyes. Zeus himself 7-foot in height equal to the being sitting. The skull twice the size as Zeus peering back. The cold dark eyes showing the reflection of the leader of the Olympus.

"This being is pure darkness" ...pacing towards the exit Zeus decided what must be done. "Destroy it."

"How can we destroy the being?" Hera questioned as Poseidon

stood ready to perform the procedure, "We don't even know what it is, or why it is here"

"It is an abomination Hera. If allowed it will tear the entire fabric of all creation suppressing it under its power. Look around you Hera, this is not Elysium. There are things within this place that I know would destroy Elysium… if not physically than the idea of Elysium. Think about this Hera, before we left to come here if anyone would have told you a force exists that could subjugate Elysium under its foot, what would you have said?"

Zeus paced around the room waiting for a reply, none came. He continued, "Impossible? It would have seemed impossible because it would have been. Standing here within the Ether, with that being there, if we were to take this being into Elysium to face Kronos, this being would devour Kronos. Think about that, the All Father. Now here is my question to you Hera…since you have been so forthright that your father doesn't know what we are dealing with, if this is also true, who is Kronos?"

Silence filled the room. Zeus looking at each one of them waiting to see if any would usurp his authority or offer a plausible explanation.

"The first thing we must do is destroy these abominations…" Before Zeus could continue his statement the ship began crashing to the left and the right as cigar shaped ships surrounded the Olympus.

The ships firing lasers onto the surface of the Olympus. The lasers having no effect other than to sway the ship to the side. It was like a wave knocking against the sides of a boat, not powerful enough to gain entry or to penetrate, but enough to make its presence aware.

"The beings have flight abilities!" Hermes announcing through the ships communication system. Zeus was even more stunned and shocked by this revelation. They were reaching out. The same as Elysium was reaching in. Was this the antithesis of Elysium? Zeus was having questions; he was seeking answers. He felt a duty to preserve the order of all things. To not allow the unknown to destroy something that had fought to extend its consciousness beyond the stars. He thought about the beings on the surface, Gods, without Godly power. What would it be like, being an eternal God, without the ability to protect yourself? The selflessness required to risk subjugation and once over run the courage to press forward against the beings that made the Gods of this place their foot stool. Zeus must find the answers.

"Send this being into the Ether." Zeus knew this creature must be destroyed.

Poseidon entering the power core of the ship knew the only way to destroy the being would be to rip it to pieces. In this place a synthesizer that recirculated the pure energy that formed the entire Ether powered the ship. The source code of life moving through the machine would pull the Titan apart one particle at a time. Removed completely from existence within Hades domain. The ultimate tool that the All Father, Kronos had placed within the ship. Did he know something that they did not? Surely he had secrets to tell. The device structured to allow the ship access into the domain of Hades. The eternal hell of all souls. Yet was it not also designed to specifically erase something from this realm. Once erased, where would it go? Away from here, and this place of confusion but where would it arrive once let go?

As the machine began the process covering the entire body of the being with a black tar. The tar penetrating the beings surface infecting it with energy. The large Titan fighting against the penetration of the Ether. A material that dissolved the matter within. The being unleashing a deep yell as it crushed under the dissolving pressure of the material. The material that surrounds the eternal hell of souls. Zeus looking out a porthole of the ship wondered, why would Kronos design something to destroy something unless he also knew that something else exists which could destroy him.

The jaw bone falling away first, the skull collapsing on itself. The being vanishing into the black substance which was

then assembled and placed into a canister to be taken for storage. A research capsule to be stored for future analysis of the material that makes up the Titans.

"Royals, we will go down and rid this planet of these abominations. They must be removed from the Ether, or the possibility exists that we may one day fall under their foot." Zeus was serious and resolute that none should remain.

The Olympus again returning to the same city positioning above the tall pyramid. The Gods of Elysium dispersing into the cities of the world to capture the Titans removing them from among the people. As the Royals traversed the world in the war against the Titans they overwhelmed the beings with advanced technology. It was not as if the process of collecting them all was as simple as collecting flowers from a rose bush. There were thorns. The beings trapped in the ether, all dissolved and imprisoned within the dark canisters for future analysis and yet Zeus wondered whether within the substance they still existed.

It could have very well been the case, the Royals arrive one layer, one click to the right or the left, in this scenario it would have been they being immobilized by these beings. More the reason why these Titans must be removed.

Zeus walking among the indigenous people who built the large city marveled. The people crowding around this bearded God as he allowed them to approach him. They mingled with the other Gods and they walked among them.

Speaking the whole time to the victors, "We will lead these people towards their destiny. In the ways of Elysium." Everyone knew that going back to Elysium would only bring more questions. They also knew Kronos would begin to wonder what they had found, what was occurring, and should he arrive the entire world would be placed in jeopardy. This was not the hell he had been told existed within the Ether. This was a heaven. A place where endless possibilities existed, where benevolence was demanded. It was a heaven that was the anti-thesis of the heaven he came from, but heaven none the less.

Sending out the Gods to the other ten cities Zeus knew his Gods would easily bind the Titans. He anticipated that complete removal of the abominations to life would occur within one planetary rotation.

His hopes were dashed when Demeter did not return from her journey to the city of the southern continent. The Royal Gods of Elysium pacing endlessly on the ship Olympus. Zeus had positioned the ship upon a high mountain overlooking the massive enclosed sea.

"Something must have happened." Aphrodite now present on the helm speaking in dismay to the other Gods. "Nothing happened Aphrodite, I am sure she just lost track of time, she will be here." Hermes trying to ease her frustration.

"Track of time? Non-sense, something has happened. You will all sit here as if everything is fine, as every moment passes Demeter may be in need of help." Aphrodite was frantic over the disappearance of Demeter.

"I am not going anywhere!" Apollo was done moving in this strange environment. He was a scientist. He was not the savior of those Gods who freely chose to make their own decisions."

Zeus resting upon the massive commander's chair. In the halls of the Olympus the throne of Zeus was a position of his status in Elysium. A reality where everything is based on hierarchy with absolute obedience to those who have been given stewardship over them. He watched bickering among the Gods, he considered their behavior that of children. Beings removed from their state of comfort, forced to face a reality that demanded they rethink their own reality. Zeus was beyond these foolish entities complaints. They failed to grasp the bigger picture. Kronos was not the answer to all things.

"Silence! Gods of Elysium no one here is free except Zeus. It is a shame that you place the burden of finding Demeter upon me or upon yourselves The blame will not fall upon us, the Gods, we who will watch over the mortal Gods on the Earth. You ask why I do not raise my finger to assist Demeter, let Demeter assist herself. My duty is to those below who look up. My duty is not to those above looking down."

The disgruntled leader storming out of the room moving into the dark corridors of the ship. He must meet with his closest advisor. He must find Jupiter. Jupiter would know what he should do about the powerless Gods on the surface of this world overwhelmed with the many creatures seeking their demise.

"Is God willing to prevent evil, but not able? Then he is not omnipotent. Is he able, but not willing? Then he is malevolent. Is he both able and willing? Then whence cometh evil? Is he neither able nor willing? Then why call him God?" – Epicurus

9

THE BROKEN GOD

Zeus could not imagine living in a world where he had no power. Mortal beings with eternal attributes without power. Zeus could hardly imagine it. It would be like stripping the sun of its rays. How could a being of omnipotence become a being without any omnipotence, and vice versa?

His mere existence defied the laws of these beings and their existence defied the laws of his existence. The source of the Ether confirming that these human beings, these mortal men, were more Gods than even himself. Zeus contemplated the thought, who should be serving who?

The grand leader now past his deadline to reach back towards the stars to Elysium, the All Father, Kronos. What would he say, what would he do? This world's existence pressing against the boundaries of time itself would either confirm what Kronos already knew and be destroyed.

He had always considered Jupiter his equal. His knowledge of the things of the Gods more extensive. He had spent greater time with the All-Father. He had himself been on many journeys into the greater and the lesser voids.

"Zeus! My All-Brother!" The large being jovially laughing as he embraces Zeus. "What brings you to this part of the Olympus? I am preparing my analysis of the material that was collected from the surface, this is very interesting."

"Jupiter, I am confused as to why these things are, the All-Father has told me that this place would be filled only with tortured souls. Souls striving to be brought forward as Royal

Ones. Surely, you have seen what I have seen?"

Jupiter could see the frustration that weighed on Zeus mind and responded accordingly. "These being's genetic foundation suggests while they are the equivalent of Kronos in this place they originate elsewhere."

"You mean; these beings were brought here?" Zeus was more confused than ever.

Jupiter responded, "Not exactly brought here, I would submit they were created here by entities from a world the same as our own."

"I knew it!" Zeus proclaiming as he turned back towards Jupiter, "Have you ever considered that while we have been viewing ourselves at the top, that we were actually at the bottom? Jupiter, my most trusted friend. I believe that Elysium is only the beginning, and not the ending. I also believe that All-Father has been lying to us."

"Zeus, such talk is blasphemous! Kronos will have you dissolved into the Ether if he ever heard you speak such a way!"

"Why is that Jupiter? Why is it expulsion? Why is it dissolution for asking why these things are so?" The God king and his closest advisor knowing the conversation about to continue would drift into areas that could cost both their lives.

"Kronos speaks of this Great Scientist, have you seen him one time? Have you met him? Hera, his own daughter says that he knows nothing, that it is all a mystery to him. If this is the case, do we not have the responsibility to seek out the answers for ourselves? Are we not of all of the creations best equipped to find the answers that elude us? If not granted out of our desire to know, a way should be granted simply because we have the ability to ask, why?" Zeus was moving among the machinery that Jupiter operated. The towers that rose up and down filled with crystals from Elysium that would organize the ships energy.

"Zeus, my All-Brother, remember that with every step towards this light, which is knowledge, the further you will wander into the void of nothingness. Beware, lest Hades swallow you whole."

"Hades?" The scowling leader stepped back, "Tell me, who is Hades? Is it a place, a person, a thing? Or is Hades, the unknown? Could Hades be the manifestation of the darkness that exists which conceals the answers to the questions? Could Hades, the father of all lies, be a similitude of the independent thought of the God within aligning himself with that which he knows to be true, which is in opposition to the forces that seek to bind and control? Tell me Jupiter, could Hades be the fears, the shadows of the heart, the mind and the soul reaching beyond the seen to create a protective barrier between the answers that do exist and the fears of the beings too afraid to ask them, to accept them? Jupiter, I am beginning to question whether Hades exists at all."

"This is Hades, Zeus, this entire realm. It is life eternal, the imprisonment of souls." Zeus did not think Jupiter knew but he respected his friend enough to listen. "With all due respect, you saw the planet with powerless Gods. You saw the material from the beings that were created here for the sole purpose of enslaving the powerless Gods. You yourself have seen these things. Things that Kronos says should not exist."

"Zeus, before you step into this direction. Know this, with every decision comes an ending. With every step a destination. With one choice the dissolution of possible outcomes, with wide ranging effects on the future. If you do this, your actions will be all-encompassing and ripple through time. Even to Elysium herself. Even to the foot stool of Kronos, the Father of Time himself. Where knowledge cannot destroy, surely Kronos can, be careful."

The two Gods ended their discussion embracing as Jupiter continued his genetic research on the black substance from the Titan and Zeus returning to the helm of the ship.

"Zeus." Jupiter calling his attention again. "I can say this for sure. I have never seen the source of any being programmed in a way that it behaved like an infection. These beings, whatever created these beings, you best avoid that encounter. We may not survive."

"Not survive?" Zeus responded, "We are Gods. We are the stewards to the fabric of time. It becomes our duty to root out the darkness, to separate it from the light."

Jupiter could see Zeus did not understand what he was saying.

He continued, "This material, if coming into contact with any bio-logical matter self-replicates. This being is not dead. This being is waiting in stasis, a genetic hibernation. Who could have created such a being? Think about that Zeus."

Zeus returned to the helm as the other ships attacking the Olympus were being destroyed. The command of the ship blast-ing the cigar shaped ships that had surrounded the Olympus with beams of pure energy. Energy directly from the source that powered through the ship. The large ships breaking under the pressure. The celestial energy disintegrating their traveling devices.

Zeus knew, "Titans!"

The Titans retreating from the behemoth titans of the sky, run by visitors walking in upon the remnants of a broken world residing within broken space and time. To protect Gods without powers and understand why these things are the way that they are and have been was Zeus mission. The constant threat Kronos may enter, may ap-pear, Zeus knew that altercation would be revealing as Kronos would be face to face with his own deceptions.

"They are retreating Zeus." Apollo stated as he and the other Gods working the ships instruments were beating them back with the celestial weaponry. "I want them all grounded." Zeus ordered throughout the ship. The ship again regaining its position on the top of the large granite mountain.

Zeus calling a congregation among the Gods. He knew the dis-cussion must occur to pull everyone in line with the reality of why they were there and what would be to come. "A short time ago, we left Elysium. Many of you for the first time. We came here at the request of the All-Father. Upon arrival we have come to the conclu-sion that All-Father has deceived us."

Hushes and whispering began spreading among the congrega-tion of Gods. Zeus continued, "Kronos deceived us. Below us on the surface of this world exist a people. Human beings the same as you and I. They are Gods, on every level the analysis they are our equals without our powers. Yet what becomes of them?"

"What do you mean what becomes of them?" Aphrodite ques-tioning Zeus. The leader looking at her with scorn, "I am not finished, do not interrupt me again. "Imagine being Gods in a world where you had no Godly powers. Where you were subject to the mercy of all other life forms. Imagine, dear Aphrodite, the selflessness of such a being. To abandon them to a life with no control, while we rest upon our mountain top looking down that we have done it all. I ask you, have you? Yet not one here has any idea what you did to deserve your place in the eternities. I call that, Irony. Who here among you has a memory of a previous existence? None. Yet is it not proclaimed throughout all of Origin it is we who have earned the reward, how can you earn something to which you have no memory? Who here has earned his Godliness? Who among you can say, it is their destiny to fail and your destiny to succeed? Who here has earned the right to say that? I will tell you Aphrodite, Hermes, Hera, what I see. I see my brothers, I see my sisters, and I see duty."

The grand leader choosing to put down his mantle, whether it was chosen for him by himself or others he would descend below all. He would be remembered for all time as the being who stood with man until the end. Who understood that only through selfless-ness could free agency be actualized. Without previous memories he would choose for himself. What greater act could he bestow upon them? To lay down his life for his friends. Zeus knew that the desti-ny of man was dependent upon his ability to assist them in a reality that was designed to sift them to the bone.

He continued, "These beings are walking on a world of un-knowns, worlds without number that would crush them if given the opportunity. The greatest of all the Gods, yet moving into the dark-ness willingly. I ask you, who are they? None within Elysium had the courage to take the steps these beings would. Who truly was the weaker God? Who was closer to transcendence? Who the Godlier? What good is power and omnipotence or free agency, if it is never used?"

Turning back to the other Gods. Zeus continued, "I will not go see Kronos, and neither will any of you. We will close the door. Kro-nos will come. Whether we go to him first or have him come here, he will come. We must prepare as many of them as possible to the destruction that will occur when Kronos comes."

"We will be cast out forever" Hera crying throwing her arms into the air.

"Cast down forever?" Zeus felt sad for the pettiness of his people. "You know not what it is to weep… one day away from Elysium is worth more time to your soul than an eternity groveling at the feet of a complacent eternal being."

Zeus was disgusted, leaving the company of the Gods. With the exception of Demeter who was still missing he knew none were prepared for what was to come. He knew very little about what he would do when Kronos arrived. Perhaps, in that moment he could plead with him to reason. Share the data, let him see first-hand. Perhaps then Kronos would not seek to destroy them all. He knew it was only a matter of time. What was time, in this world it was irrelevant. What was ten million years' worth of work to have Kronos appear with legions mere seconds after he left? He was assuming the God of Time was focused on other things, but the moment he would question, would be the moment he would arrive. Zeus was surprised he hadn't arrived yet.

Yet this was the truth.

He must polish them up, make them seem so refined that not even Kronos could deny their value to Elysium. The first thing he needed to do was rid the planet of all other unnecessary life. With the existence of the giants and the many hostile beasts, as well as all those things left behind, Zeus knew there would need to be a dramatic cleansing.

Zeus had an idea. He would need the help of Poseidon to pull that off. Poseidon, the master of all elements. He always knew the answers to the questions that Zeus did not. Especially in this foreign place, the Kingdom of Hades.

Reentering the engineering corridor Jupiter was moving crystals from one tower to the next. "Poseidon, Poseidon, we will flood the Earth. It's the only way. We will begin now extracting as many as possible. However, we must flood the Earth." Jupiter was startled at Zeus entrance into the room speaking nonstop.

"Flood the Earth?" The scientist replied, "You do realize this requires water, massive amounts of water, where do you supposed we get all that water?"

Laughing to himself Zeus replied, "Poseidon, humor me, come, take a ride with me, I would like to show you something that we have overlooked."

Taking a smaller ship from the Olympus out into the outer atmosphere. Zeus was able to show Poseidon massive icebergs the size of small moons floating in orbit around the Earth. Jupiter remembered the barrier of ice that circled the planet. "Zeus, this might actually be an idea!"

"I have theorized that this ice came from the oceans of the neighboring planet we saw as we approached this world. They have remained in an orbit around this planet. There is more water floating around this planet than currently on the world. What I need to know, how do we move them?"

Poseidon looking around became quiet as he processed the puzzle. "There is a velocity, the point where these objects will no longer orbit but will descend. We can nudge the objects slightly sending them past this threshold into the atmosphere where they will burn forming condensation in the atmosphere showering the world in an unending sea of water. We could use the tractor beam on the Olympus. We could fly around the planet sending enough towards the surface that none would be prepared." Poseidon was convinced that this would work.

The mind of Zeus reeling with the possibilities. Calling a gathering of the Gods he approached them with his idea to cleanse the Earth of the filth that bogged her down.

"Gods and goddesses, watchmen of mankind, the decision has been made to rid the Earth of the darkness that possesses its soul. In the coming days the rain will begin. Once the rain begins it will not stop until the entire face of the planet is wiped clean. Some of you may think of me as a tyrant, cruel, and uncaring. Consider this, when Kronos arrives, will your feelings matter to him in your moment of judgement? You have one goal between now and then, remove as many of the humans as you can. Leave the mutants alone, you know who to retrieve and those to warn. With haste disperse to the four corners of the world."

Silence across the great hall, none moving, and none responding. Zeus had made his decision. He could care less

what the spoiled children of Elysium thought about the decision. He knew many of them would be devastated to lose their access to manipulate the common people of the planet. They worshiped the praise of the people. Pulling the strings of the puppets simply to be adorned.

While Zeus knew they protected the mortals from the evils of the landscape below and those from the stars above many of them just did not get it. He had thought about the hundreds of years they had been among the people. How much had they done? Instead of teaching the people about what is coming, the Gods using the time to philander, pillage and elevate themselves. Enough was enough. It was time for a rest. After all, this world clearly had been reset many times before.

The large Olympus filled with ten thousand humans from the planet's surface. There were many others that had been warned to prepare. There were those who chose to continue in their ways living in the cities built by the Titans. The planet truly belonged to the Titans but that would soon end. The cross culture of crippled broken Gods fighting to hang on to a relic slowly slipping away.

The Gods of Elysium moved around the planet sending the massive icebergs descending into the Earth's atmosphere. For forty days the Gods pummeled the Earth's atmosphere with the collection of Mars ocean ice which had been trapped in the atmosphere for thousands of years. Zeus had pondered how this lost world had come to be and why it was that this world's oceans had become trapped around the Earth.

The ice waiting for the free agency that could only be made by the Gods to allow it entry into the Earth. The planet a raging ocean. The Earth pounded by mile high waves rolling around the planet. Among the waves large vessels made by inhabitants. Zeus had felt, if those beings whether human or otherwise were wise enough to build arks to survive the deluge, they were deserving of a life in the new world. These were the type of ruggedly determined doers he was looking for, those willing to go against the grain of the culture now lying at the bottom of the ocean floor.

The culture of the Titans was stripped from the surface of the planet. The Titans forced into submission within the womb of the world. Swallowing them up the Titans permanently imprisoned within the belly of the Earth. It would be impossible for the Eternal beings to remove themselves from such depths, imprisoned for all time, or for a time, from the affairs of men.

Those separated from the rest residing on Olympus and within the vessels floating across the Earth sifted as wheat, groomed and taught by the Gods. Welcomed into their abode. They were treated as Gods, equal with the Gods. This was the decree of Zeus. This was the time the humans were taught culture, mathematics, language, literature, and the arts. They were showed agriculture and commerce. The things necessary in the world to come to be welcomed by the Gods, who were yet to come.

Zeus always saying, "It is better to prepare now for the appearance of those from on high, then to arise asleep when they have passed you by." Zeus knew this was a one shot deal. If his strategy to adjust human beings to the life of Elysium failed, they were already dead. If it worked, he may buy this species the time necessary to achieve whatever potential the cruel ethos thrust upon them as they rest in the heart of the inferno itself.

As the planet recovered from the deluge the receding waters revealed Earth void of all life. No buildings, no large cities, and no massive lizards hunting man in the forests. No Titans or Lizard Men, no shape shifters. The surface of the Earth was refreshed, purified, all things buried beneath. There were also survivors.

As the Olympus covered the surface of the Earth, the mountain cliffs were covered with survivors. Zeus marveled, he had followed through with his commitment however, mother Earth had shown him that even she could show mercy. Arks of life littered mountain tops across the globe. In one way or another he contemplated the thought that there were others like himself also aware of what needed to be done. It was a theory. The helm of Olympus resting on a mighty mountain overlooking a peaceful bay in a portion of the world that would support the survivors within Olympus who he commanded to multiply and replenish the surface.

Zeus had thought about visiting every Ark, seeking their story, but he chose not to for one reason. Who was he to determine which Gods chose to interact on their being's behalf or not?

He would do his part, if there were others also doing their part that he was unaware, then let them do their part for their own purposes. Knowledge of the genie in the bottle would take the fun of asking for wishes. Zeus knew this, when he was completed this world would be covered in Gods who freely choose to live as the Gods do. Rising freely to his very throne. Demonstrating a trust and a loyalty between them and himself he believed in humanity. He was preparing the people of the Earth for a time when they would become greater than himself. That foundation a necessary step that someone would have to take, why not him?

With the massive sheets of ice removed from the planet's atmosphere, the surface of the world became a more stable environment. The oceans refreshed and renewed. The pollution of the Titans removed. The surface replenished with vegetation, the health of the entire eco system improved. Zeus knew it was almost too late, the Titans nearly devouring the world and all those on its surface. The flood was the only way to compete with their genetic manipulation expertise. These beings had the power to manipulate matter, to create life, which was not a crime unless it meant the end of humanity.

Even Zeus and the other Gods from Elysium did not know how to create a life from DNA. None had even seen DNA. Yet as they destroyed these creatures they would reappear with the ability to reanimate themselves producing millions of their kind across the surface. Abandoned themselves upon the surface of the planet they only sought to rule, forcing the people to conform to their technology preparing for the day when their own great God would return.

Zeus had heard the stories about the ancient wars. The confrontations of beings from the outer Ethos entering the Earth to commune. This singular world, identified to the many, the diamond pulled from the pit in the midst of a thousand thieves. The most noble intentions turning bad, the shifting sands of the hour glass that favored none and shown mercy to only the conquered. That mercy was slavery. He had many things to worry about after the flood. The leader of a collection of eternal beings that themselves could not keep from allowing the people to worship them, the lizard man living in the southern hemisphere who had flooded the human population with his own creation of human beings. The possible arrival of the creators of the Titans. How will they react when they find the planet terra formed, when they find their high rulers deceased? When there are no Titans to greet them. How would Kronos react?

He was playing God here but in the moment of decision when in-decision would have eternal ramifications he would be the first one to strike fear into man to ensure they knew their place in the Cosmos. He had done that, if anything to have proper respect for the horrors that would be coming their way. The flood had been that message. Obviously the message got around, there were large pockets of the planets human population that survived. They remember and those first few generation that will step foot onto the replenished Earth will be grateful. Zeus groaned within his heart, he knew that this would be the final time he would assume the mantle of decision maker over who deserves to live and who deserves to die.

The flood had been emotionally difficult for him to follow through. He struggled with the decision to wipe many bits of intelligence from the globe, to behave as though he knew better. He knew the common good and therefore it was done…it made him feel as close to the being Kronos as he dared go. He could not do that to a planet again. In a reality where multiple levels of Gods would be interacting with one world, confusing the potluck of human history with myth, fable, and fantasy he would want the world to know nothing less than this,

"He did what he thought was right. He did it out of love. He did it out of fear. He did not wish to harm, he did not wish to rule, he wished to protect. Protect all life and all humanity. If he could speak to those that were lost, the Titans, the Lizards, the hybrids of life that flooded the Earth it would be to say that he was sorry. He was sorry for having to be the one to remove them from the Earth. It was not out of hate, to destroy, or for personal gain. It was out of love for something that was weak, that unless these beings made their sacrifice would have perished."

Most of all if Zeus could speak to the Mother Earth that received another planets nourishment would say, "I am sorry that you have been alone. I am sorry that the people of this planet have used you, captivated you, stripped you of your life, I am sorry that you have been alone. I have brought you the nourishment of your sister who had given her life to nourish you. I pray they do not do as the Titans had done and devour her once more."

If Zeus were in that moment, if he had that chance to have the words of his mouth echoed through time. Written by men through generations it would be that they do not judge him by what he had to do, that they judge him by the men that he helped to make through the choices that he had to make. There are no easy decisions when making decisions which life deserves to be preserved. The greatest goal of Zeus in that moment would be the future ages when the men of the Earth would surpass even himself.

In that moment rising up, unshackling themselves from the Earth and tearing down all of his statues and monuments refusing to accept him as a God. To realize for themselves in that the master was not greater than the servant. That Zeus was not a God living among men, he was a man living among Gods.

"To see a world in a grain of sand and heaven in a wild flower Hold infinity in the palms of your hand and eternity in an hour."
-William Blake

10

GREAT SCIENTIST

The rain had begun falling and it had never let up. The mountain caverns a refuge for the inhabitants of the Anasazi and the people of Ares. Michael and Kulkukan strategizing in the ship contained within a large mountain as to the fate of the planet once the floodwaters would recede.

"How can the rain simply fall day after day?" A bewildered Michael spoke as Kulkukan pondered the question. "It has been raining for thirty straight days. The floodwaters have submerged the cavern entrance. We can't even leave or else the barrier will be broken flooding the cavity. Shouldn't we at least evacuate the cavern to bring everyone on board the ship, just in case?"

"Michael" the old man seeking wisdom to calm the anxiety boiling over with Michael. "Can you not see, Gia is being reborn, when the flood waters recede a new world will remain, a new place, called Earth."

"Earth?" Michael questioning, that's my world you are referencing. "Yes, Earth, a new age of man is beginning. One where those who strive to reach the mountain top will have a fair opportunity of achieving that goal. In what other scenario could it have been possible to wipe the planet from the geneticist gone mad, the Titans? A species gone mad with time, resorting to eating those beings that they created on the surface. It is better this world never know of their horrors."

The Old Man speaking as if he knew this one species would be best erased from all of the Earth's history. "When you first arrived Michael, you asked why? You sought for the answers that lay just beyond the horizon of your mind. You faced the darkness of yourself pressing against those limits seeking further light and knowledge. The answers scattered around you as a puzzle tossed into the air by the wind. Having the courage to work piece by piece through the puzzle. To accept new insight, and new ideas, to have the confidence to try again when the darkness consumed you in your madness to reach the source of all. Beginning at the bottom, the master becoming the servant. Understanding that the only way to escape is to look within. By looking within the keyhole to exit the dark tower that clouds your mind becomes visible."

Michael standing in silence as the great leader continued to express his thoughts, feelings, and ideas. A part of him knew, this was the time to listen.

"You have traveled through the doorway of time, without this the proper order of the story would have become lost. Diluted. Forgotten. You are the answer to your own question. When the onion layers are peeled back, when you see as the Gods see, when you realize that it is they who all look to you. Only then will you realize that the illusion of reality is no illusion at all, it is a gateway for escape."

"Escape from what?" Michael asked

The Old Man pondering his words knowing that the future destiny of this one man, this one singular being who had been so instrumental in the development of the story to this point would depend on his ability to be the storyteller.

Michael, let me ask you a question, "If you realized upon birth the true nature of the game of life, would you not see the trivial nature that this life within this simulated world is merely an illusion. This alone making death merely an illusion, a God in a temporary space, would you not in this moment with this understanding stand up and kill yourself instantly to escape the illusion of reality? You see Michael, you would be as the Gods, knowing that there is no death but only life and rebirth. Yet, to progress out of the labyrinth of souls that leads to the beginning of the next chapter requires a willing submission to the game of life. Only then can you approach the doorway beyond the Ethos, which we are now enclosed. You spend your whole life stuck in the labyrinth, thinking about how you'll escape one day. Imagining that future is what keeps you going, but you never do it. Not because of a lack of desire but because in the moment of entering the grand ballroom emerging at the apex of the entire system with no memory. In the end it always comes back to free agency, the requirement for the independent decision to do what is necessary to transcend. On one hand, a God looking up with no power. On the other, a God looking down with power. Both beings trapped inside the same sifter of souls."

Kulkukan opened his arms like a large circle. "The future of this planet, these people of mine and Ares people, all those who would choose to enter within is dependent upon the storytellers who write the lines of the chapters still to come. This is one of the two great mysteries into which human minds are drawn. The question of free will versus predestination and what to do when starting back at the beginning."

The Old Man leading Michael out of the ship into the long cavern which housed his people, Ares people and all those they could warn prior to the flood's beginning. Caverns continually hollowed out of the massive mountain with animals, food, and seeds of all kind. This truly was an ark.

What was an ark? If nothing more than a storage device preserving that which would be lost to the fabric of time. Cataclysm fosters progression from one life to the next the ability to retain previous knowledge is a great gift. Kulkukan knew the human mind was the ark.

"What will become of Ares and his people once the flood is over?" Michael questioned.

"They will be grafted into our own. No doubt their struggle to arrive will be forgotten to time. The roots of their tree and the roots of our own merged as if one. Becoming one flesh, one body, one people. They have earned that right. You however do not belong here." The inquisitive Old Man turning to face Michael.

"The world to come will be faced with many dangers, many unknowns, and as you and I know, its future is not guaranteed. But there are those watching, those looking down upon us now. From without the Ethos of the world in which we are all bound that lies within the void of darkness. It is too them that we look for strength and the courage to do that which will be difficult. The courage to accept one's fate, to live according to it, to choose to leave the story only when the story has ended for you. There is a way that you can escape this place."

Looking Michael into the eyes, placing his hands upon his shoulders, the Old Man, Kulkukan again spoke. "I would like to show you something."

Leading Michael through one of the long corridors that had been carved into the mountain. The two walking through dwellings etched into the cliffs. An entire culture hidden within the Earth. This was the new beginning that he needed. More than anything Michael just wondered if he had done enough to prevent the future attack from occurring. He had seen the great flood with his own eyes and it was far worse than the book proclaimed. Could he stop the future attack or would he be trapped in the past forever? The human time traveler weary from the journey and overwhelmed by the truth just wanted to go home.

They stopped in a massive atrium in the midst of a lone Tulip Tree.

"This is our most prized possession. The last Tulip Tree in this entire world. Observe its beauty, how the pink flowers open to welcome the honey bee."

Looking closely, Michael could see the tree surrounded by honeybees. Millions of bees flying in and out of the buds of the Tulips which covered the span of the trees canopy, limbs, and base.

"What is the honey bees function here?" The Old Man questioning Michael.

"To get honey for the bee hive." Responding Michael.

"Yes, the function of the bee is to perform its duty with the time given to it to collect pollen. Which it takes back to the hive where it is processed. It is the responsibility of every honey bee. Does the honey bee question its duty to the hive? Does the honeybee question its directive? Is there a singular person, place, or thing that can be measured, quantified to explain how the honey bee knows what it is to do in life, how it is to accomplish this function? How do they know?"

The old man now standing within the sea of deep pink variations of the tulips. The bees flying by and through his arms and around Michael.

"This is the answer to the mystery of answering the question why. To and fro, away they go. To universes of plenty among a sea of the many. Unaware. Of what would be out there. Yet the bee fulfills its life in the transition of processing material and where does it go? Imagine the bee stopping in its journey and asking to itself, why?"

"Has a bee in existence ever stopped and asked itself why? I would suppose so. Would the bee with its understanding of the micro pollen to the macro Tulip tree? Beyond the yard, the block, the valley, the region, the continent, the planet, the solar system, the galaxy, the universe, the sea that provides the great Ethos of Spheres, to the honey combs upon honey combs of systems of fishing of souls, at what point is the honey bee capable of understanding? Imagine the human life the equivalent of the honey bee in a sea of information so vast that the reality of its existence would be meaningless and yet without the human life there would be no transportation for the honey towards the source of time itself. Without the honey bee there exists no eco system. The Tulips themselves universes upon universes of life. To the sub atomic level, the unseen of the unseen the worlds of existence isolated and unknowing of the being to which they are forever linked, the consciousness of the plant. The eternity of time within those worlds between the moments of the buds opening, closing, and falling away. Not measured in time as we know it, but in time on a micro level equal to billions, if not trillions of years."

Opening one of the pink tulips. The old man lifted his finger to show pollen covering his finger.

"Within each of these bits of intelligence, the pollen that is essential for honey, are universes upon universes. How many of any of these have ever questioned why? Perhaps none. All these universes unaware of the honey bees coming and going. Distributing the pollen to the hive where it is processed for the creation of an eternal resource, honey. The honey bee unaware of the sparrows flying by that pluck them from the sky. Without the bee the flower would not bloom. The bloom would wither and die. The tree's ability to obtain nourishment compromised. From the tulip to the root the tree would die. From every level of existence the meaning of life can be derived from watching the honey bee move about the tulip tree in a cosmic sea of expanses. Sometimes we are the flower, sometimes we are the leaves, sometimes we are the honey bee flying through the tree, sometimes we are the branches strong and true, and sometimes we are the pollen carried beyond all that we knew."

"The meaning of life is to serve...To love that around you...to give of yourself wherever you are able to assist. The meaning of life is to be a respecter of the worlds that exist all around you that with the swipe of a hand are erased from time and history and sometimes to be the pollen never questioning your essential need in all of creation. If you saw the maze for what it truly was and were capable of comprehending its labyrinth, you would see that it is better to find a place to hide than seek for answers that may be too difficult to accept. You would see the importance of serving them. If you were pulled from the fish pond taken beyond the grove, into the universe, through the many levels of creation, you would gasp for air and wish to return. Michael, what would be the point of the honey bee becoming aware of the entire universe around it if it came at the expense of the pollen not being delivered and the entire system crumble to pieces? At what price is knowledge? The entire perspective of time relative to yourself and to the bee, this tree, its eco system is to understand the process of creation. Am I wiser than you?" The old man paused expecting an answer.

Michael stood motionless. The old man, Kulkukan, the immortal leader of the Anasazi, forever chained to this universe by choice. Michael amazed that he would choose to stay upon realizing the greater purpose of it all. Choosing to serve than to travel to unknown worlds in a greater sea of life. He dared not answer the ancient being, knowing that to make an attempt would be seen as either patronizing or groveling.

"If you choose to live out your life as the universe has intended, here in this time, among these people knowing what you now know, you would be wiser than I am. You could be a honey bee here among these people. There is a great culture coming to this world. A growth, a collaboration of the eternals upon this world to serve the weak, to lift the helpless, to be among the great Gods of all creation. Ponder upon that, among the great Gods of all creation. Knowledge is about to be poured out upon it, those above looking down upon those below. Serving the mortal Gods. You can help guide these people with your wisdom, and knowledge. To find knowledge in the beginning of the first new society on the Earth."

Walking back to the tree Kulkukan held the leaves of the flower between his fingers, the thumb and the index with leaves presses through the ring and pinky.

"Your life should be the bushel of leaves, the collection of family and friends. That nourishment bringing into existence beautiful new tulips. The self-manifestation of perfection. What makes man so great is his beginning, the perfect imperfection, the mortal god who must trust to survive. At the end of the road, when the sun sets, what matters most? I will tell you, it's a beautiful day indeed when the sun rises."

Michael stopping to the last statement remembering the comment from the source before he arrived on Tiamat. Michael chose to stay rather than leave. As the years progressed vast intellectual civilizations covered the globe. From the north to the south, the east to the west humanity from all continents meeting, interacting, grafting each other's peoples, cultures and knowledge. The species became one people from one world.

The age of man had arrived.

As time progressed so the world passed him by, the young man aging with the wind until grey hair and wrinkles the old man was nearing the end of his life. Thinking about the years that had passed. How long they had seemed. The stories of the past nothing more than fables, fairy tales, and fantasies. Too unbelievable to be true, too absurd in the structured order of this time. Refinement, idealism, community gathering.

The people of the Earth striving to reach for the stars to run with the gods. Zeus and his pantheon walking among them. One last visit to impart wisdom before it would be time to go. To speak with an old man living high above the village on a hill hidden within the sky. The wisest man in the world, Peto.

He had a gift to impart before his final journey to see his old friend Kulkukan who had summoned him. The seeker becoming the finder, the imparter of truth knew his time on the Earth was coming to an end.

Held within his hands a golden looking glass, a gift to the man on the hill. Would show him the planets, stars, it would remove the heavenly veil. This man would see as Gods from beginning to end offering a way to leave. The secret of the gift to the wisest man who lived on the hill, an instrument that was created that allowed the man the ability to leave the game.

For centuries the old man had the ability to leave but chose instead submission to the game called life. To be the bee who never questioned why and just lived his life as was expected. To live the life given to him, waiting until the time to give away this instrument would come. He moved slowly with painstaking effort, step by step until he reached the summit. There he approached the man on the hill. Saying nothing, he simply handed Peto the looking glass, turned and walked away. The wise man on the hill choosing to leave rather than stay, the old man continuing on his journey grateful he was given another day.

After three days' journey Michael came to the great mountain where Kulkukan resided. Climbing the final steps up the trail to the mountain side the old man found the entrance to the ancient city deep inside. In solemn reverence all had heard of his coming and assembled to welcome him into the abode of Kulkukan. Upon seeing Kulkukan he marveled that he hadn't aged in over 90 years. Michael now frail, aged, with time long passing him by, he was meeting Kulkukan for the last time. Michael was preparing to die.

The two laughed about their memories, how the people had already forgot all that had occurred. Perhaps for the best it was what they deserved.

He lay in Kulkukan study knowing his moment was near. As Michael lay dying about to give his last breath. He asked Kulkukan the question about what happens next. Kulkukan, rising to his feet, "Michael my dear friend, I have something to share I am so glad we meet again. Since you have been gone I have recalibrated the machine left behind by Mastem. I have something you have to see. A doorway to the source of all creation. The stairway to the Great Scientist himself, the key to be free."

The old man barely able to walk assisted along by his eternal native friend knew this was the end. Michael approaching to view the machine that had once been a part of a story long ago. Kulkukan working to turn the machine on. It blasted a beam of energy into the wall that tore the fabric of space open revealing a singular black door. The black door neatly framed against a dark ocean of nothing. The door handle neat, shiny and silver. Michael could also see his reflection in the windows on the door. The six window panes tinted so that he could not see through to the other side.

"Why is this door here?" The old man asked Kulkukan.

"I know, I have asked the same question time and time again. It is the beginning of everything, a doorway, as easy as that. I am not sure there really needs to be a reasoning."

"Do we open the door, it's almost too good to be true" Michael questioned Kulkukan. "I think that's your decision to make. In your frail age with nothing to lose wouldn't it be something if it were as simple as turning the handle and opening the door?" Kulkukan seemed pleased and delighted at what lay before his friend Michael.

"Have you opened the door?" Questioned Michael.

Kulkukan remained silent. Michael thinking to himself, "One more journey into the unknown, it had been so long, this might be something he would enjoy." He had lived his life, he knew this was the case, in fact he was sure this journey to Kulkukan would be his last for he had given up the sacred looking glass.

"I will open the door. I will go inside. I will meet this great scientist before I die." Grasping Kulkukan in a long embrace, he moved to the door that loomed beyond the ripple in the matrix of time.

Twisting the handle, he pushed the door open revealing a circular room made of brick. He stepped in closing the door behind him. The room was dimly lit. There were no sources of light yet he could see the brick stone forming the walls that rose endlessly upwards. In the middle of the room a staircase that rose up into the darkness at the top of the towering room. It was like climbing a lighthouse. He would have to walk the final steps alone. Climbing the spiral staircase placed in this location for God knows what reasoning. For the one or the many who find their way to the dark tower that leads to the Great Scientist it would be a journey traveled alone. The wizard behind the looking glass peering down as the twisted versions of reality spin endlessly and yet in perfect harmony. The story woven through time artfully. Would this being be the oppressive all powerful Kronos who had yet to return to the Earth?

Yet, only moments had passed in Origin. He had been from the future; he knew at some point Kronos had to come back. Would this stairway lead all the way to Kronos? Would it emerge in his personal hall of torture? Would it lead to Vorigon? Where was that vile beast? He knew Mastem had left to find Dyaus. The events to occur, the emergence of that dark being, too much story left to tell. Could this stairway lead to the darkest of forces meant to lure the foolish to death? An eternal full proof against those few who would stray, perhaps that was what was waiting at the top. Or would this Hades of Zeus, the demon forces of the underworld be waiting in Dante's Inferno delight with eternal punishments in the wheel of death for ever lost to time?

Would the dark being himself be waiting at the summit, to escort him to a special place reserved for those who broke the rules, the ambitious who sought to obtain the knowledge of the Gods? Or would Nergal the master trickster have planned an elaborate sabotage infiltrating the underground base, pretending to be Kulkukan to send him to his waiting fate. Nergal was a true god of the game called war, with long term strategy he could very well win the war. Would he be waiting at the top to unleash his revenge?

The winding of the stairs turning higher and higher they went. The slow stepping of the old man's feet the struggle to ascend. He was barely able to hold himself up but he would not miss this moment for the world. He was near the conclusion of a lifetime search to the answer of the greatest story. The story the journey did not tell of a cosmic world in a broken universe with fearful gods living everywhere. Of a world within a world of life and a cosmology of all things either one degree to the left or to the right most often in despair.

He could see the top; it was just in sight. The stairway near its crest a doorway was in sight. A brick ceiling stopped the climb as there was another closed door at the top of the winding staircase. Is this the door that led to the Great Scientist who was the source of the code that produced the world that they existed within?

Twisting the handle and opening the door, Michael stepped quietly into a room. It was a room much like the one he remembered when he was a little boy. With a window that overlooked the spacious front yard and the bookshelf that rose high against the wall in his grandfather's study. He was somewhere he had been before in a place that meant much more.

In the center of the room a large empty book lay open with a pen across its pages. Caught up in the memory of a memory Michael didn't take the time to look in the mirror. Staring in awe, no longer the old man, he was only a boy maybe nine or ten. In an instant the once familiar room spinning in circles around him shifting to mirrors showing his own reflection. The reflection of a boy looking back at himself. The mirrors still spinning in circles where the room once stood.

The imagery changing to an endless see of men in black hovering in the distance. The spinning of the mirrors continuing faster and faster until merging to produce one man in black staring back at Michael. The glass twisting as if turned in the hands of time until all the imagery resembling a kaleidoscope with fractured images of the man in black staring back at him. The spinning and twisting continuing as the room flung upside down with Michael hovering silently in the air. Bolts of electricity bursting forward through the glass until it shattered. Michael alone in the darkness of space and time spinning all around him. The darkness pressing in until the light became dim until he could not see.

Bursting forward Michael reached for the device that covered his eyes. Ripping the massive unit strapped to his head off and throwing it to the ground. Pulling a long hose out of his mouth he stood alone on a foreign ground.

Coughing up purple sludge he looked around to see where he had come. Massive and extending in all directions glowing blue beings all sitting in a bathtub like cocoon with tentacles strapped to their heads, eyes filled the megalithic realm. The entire room filled with millions of other blue beings all connected in the same way. The sound of a loud trumpet carrying slowly through the air.

Michael looking down at his hands, they were blue. In fact, he had five fingers and a thumb. Black smooth obsidian covered the floor. Puddles of water spilling out of the cocoons he could see in his reflection, he was a bald blue being with solid white eyes.

What had happened? Where was he? Where was the Great Scientist?

Rising to his feet he began the slow walk past the millions extending into all directions in a room so vast it was overwhelming. Michael noticing a small doorway that led to something below. It was an exit to something underneath.

Stepping slowly through the thirty-foot hallway he was confused and disorientated. Dripping with the purple slime that covered his body he wondered, had he risen within a harvesting facility. Was this a harvesting facility?

Michael was confused, his head ringing with the echo of the

trumpet roaring slowly through the air. The sound ominous of doom. He was still having difficulty adjusting to the bright light. Yet the room was dim, it was as if he was seeing for the very first time. He walked slowly leaning several times against the wall.

Coming to the edge of a ramp the distance below was cosmic in scale. To describe, an entire planets worth of bodies perhaps stretching an entire solar system in all directions. How else could he explain what he was seeing? Perhaps an entire galaxy of the same pods, each filled with the same blue beings in all directions.

Giant squid looking creatures floated through the air moving around the bodies grooming them, moving them, devouring them, carrying them away. He had to figure this out or else he faced certain death.

Moving back towards the room he had just come from the only thing he could do was walk endlessly across fields of bodies in cocoons. Nothing else but openings in the sky that revealed entry to other places the same as the one he walked through.

Would this be the journey to the Great Scientist? The next level of awakening into a reality that few could accept, let alone face. He had dared open Pandora's Box. He had dared see things the way they are, have been, and always will be. He had challenged time itself, pressed against the precipice of knowledge within a reality he knew was not even real. Awoken, rising from the illusion stepping forward into the true unknown. He knew could lead to his own destruction.

Looking around at the sea of trapped souls, he was meaningless in the scope of what lay all around him. The beings extending horizon to horizon in a reality where it would seem Michael was walking amongst the Sleeping Gods.

"We're born alone, we live alone, and we die alone. Only through our love and friendship can we create the illusion for the moment that we're not alone." -Orson Welles

www.ingramcontent.com/pod-product-compliance
Lightning Source LLC
Chambersburg PA
CBHW071401170626
46811CB00003B/1222